15-

MEN
IN TROUBLE

MEN
IN TROUBLE

Sarah Payne Stuart

1817

Harper & Row, Publishers, New York

Cambridge, Philadelphia, San Francisco, Washington
London, Mexico City, São Paulo, Singapore, Sydney

FIRST EDITION

Copyeditor: Bitite Vinklers
Designer: Erich Hobbing

Library of Congress Cataloging-in-Publication Data

Stuart, Sarah Payne.
  Men in trouble.

  I. Title.
PS3569.T826M46   1988   813'.54   87-45672
ISBN 0-06-015883-2

---

88 89 90 91 92 HC 10 9 8 7 6 5 4 3 2 1

To my mother and father,
and to Johnny

I would like to thank Sandy Frazier, Alan Kahn, Patty Marx, Hunter Payne, William Payne, Gregory Pilkington, John L'heureux, and Charlie Stuart for all their help with this book, and also, most especially, for making this book a hundred times better than it was, my editor and agents, Rick Kot, Liz Darhansoff, and Abigail Thomas.

MEN
IN TROUBLE

Chapter One

Then it was fall again and Harry was coming home for Sunday dinners and nobody could get a word in edgewise, my father would groan. Harry was out of the hospital now and living in some slummy apartment in Porter Square, editing math books for a Boston publisher and playing jazz in the local bars to support himself, with no plans of returning to college. He'd put on about thirty pounds since he'd been away and grown a beard and his short, neat hairdo was now a Brillo pad of fuzz that flopped up and down when he walked, and instead of black Barry Goldwater glasses, he wore smudgy Ben Franklins, which he was always wiping to no avail on his colored T-shirts. Harry would arrive around two on Sundays—we ate at two and he hated waiting around for the parents to have their one cocktail—a big sloppy bear on his 750 Norton motorcycle with his instruments strapped onto the back. Harry played three kinds of sax and two kinds of clarinet, and he couldn't go to the drugstore for aspirin without all of them with him, just in case.

We were eating in the dining room now. This was my big idea—I was fourteen and always trying to make things nice—

and every night and Sunday noon I would set the table with the little silver baskets for salt and the lace place mats and anything else I could find in the dining-room cupboards, and if it was evening, I would turn out the lights and light the candles in the silver candlesticks, which I couldn't get away with whenever Harry showed up because Harry liked to see his food when he ate.

The table looked beautiful, I must say, although the dinners themselves were not exactly affairs of elegance. The parents looked nice, of course. The parents always looked nice, especially on Sundays when they had just come from church. This was 1965, a year before the parents discovered the Vietnam War and switched to the Unitarian Church, which was so liberal you didn't have to go. I looked all right, still in what Spencer called my conformist period, dressed in pressed slacks and a flip, but Harry was a wreck, and Spencer, once a preppy dresser, now only wore blue work shirts and tan corduroys, of which he had four identical sets. "Your uniforms are washed," my mother would call up the stairs.

Spencer, who was a senior in high school, had suddenly grown bitter after a trip bicycling around Europe that summer and had arrived home wearing a troubled look and a bush of hair. ("Whose hair is longer, Spencer's or Lizzie's?" my father would ask humorously every single night.) Spencer smoked cigarettes all day and refused to mow the lawn because it was bourgeois, and there was no longer any talk of Spencer's having "the best disposition in the family."

George, who was twenty-one, was in graduate school in musicology in New York and never around, but even George didn't look so great when he was around, wearing sometimes a madras shirt with a different madras pair of shorts and a different madras belt. George was the sweetest guy in the world—gone were the days of him stomping out the front door because someone had *deliberately* stolen his razor—and happily would he have worn whatever was necessary to please the parents, but when it came to clothes he had no taste.

2

Anyway, 1965 was the second year in a row the parents didn't send out picture Christmas cards.

"I'll send out cards again when everyone starts looking better," my mother said, but it was a long, long time before she did.

"I'd kick Audrey Hepburn out of bed," Harry would announce to the stony faces of the parents, as he reached way across the table for more butter. Harry liked his women with meat on their bones, we were interested in learning. We learned a great deal about Harry's sex life that fall and usually there'd be a fight on just as it was time to do the dishes, which we suspected was no accident. Harry would stand at the sink swishing the cloth, yelling at the parents and Spencer would mention why didn't he do something with the cloth besides swishing it, and Harry would either charge out the door or start playing his saxophone so nobody could hear anything anyone else was saying. Harry didn't play Dixieland clarinet anymore, but a wild John Coltrane sax.

All my brothers were musicians—Harry's and Spencer's careers commencing the day my father called, long distance, Tommy Henrich, the Yankee right fielder he'd somehow happened to meet after a baseball game, and placed the phone next to Harry on ukulele and Spencer in diapers on maracas, singing "All day, all night, Maryanne, down by the seaside, sifting sand." "Ours is to listen," my mother would say years later when I'd come home from school to three kinds of music blaring all over the house, though sometimes my father would drag her in to sing the melody, and I'd hear her custard pudding voice rising in the midst of my father and brothers' fighting to outharmonize one another.

For a brief, torturous period, even I was a musician, my fervid, fruitless flute practicing confined to the fifteen frantic minutes that preceded my lesson every week, but then you just about had to be a musician growing up in Concord, Massachusetts, because the Concord public school system made everyone pick an instrument in fourth grade and choose either the band or the orchestra. I'd been third flute in the band, along with Nickie Oster, whose arm was too short to reach low C, and when it had come to anything tricky I'd simply taken rests. I'd picked the band because you should have heard the orchestra with all those violins. The parents would all come to assembly and the curtain would rise and there'd be this terrible screeching like a traffic jam and then the curtain would fall and everyone would clap.

In the 1960s, the Concord school system was, like the public school system of just about everyone I have ever met, one of the top ten in the country. They did all kinds of innovative things like only making us salute the flag on Wednesdays and having the students watch the teacher on TV while the teacher sat in the back of the class. Instead of history and geography, we studied The Negro and The Culture of Poverty, and to this day I cannot tell you the difference between North Dakota and South Dakota. Everybody felt pretty good about The Negro, until they bused in the blacks from South Boston and there were all kinds of rumbles. I think the parents were expecting it to be like the American Field Service, where foreign kids came to our country and had cookouts.

In Concord, the rich were careful not to be too comfortable and had the shabbiest houses and never sent their children to Europe before age sixteen. Old Mrs. Rent, who was in her eighties and must have been worth about ten mill., hung her paper towels out to dry and shoveled her driveway during snowstorms wearing, to save her 'do, a cardboard box over her head with a Saran Wrap window in the front. The intellectuals lived in the woodsy, modern part of town, and had cube puzzles and black-and-white photography books on their glass coffee tables. The fathers all worked at MIT doing something with atoms and were never at home. "I sure wish I were a genius so I wouldn't have to drive car pools," my father always

4

used to say. Then there were the people who weren't rich or intellectual, who had kids named Darlene, Marlene, and Raylene, with whom you were best friends until the school decided who was going to college and who wasn't, and then you hardly had any best friends because all the girls in your unit had straight, lank hair and went to the library after school instead of going to the five-and-ten to eat French fries with ketchup out of a paper cone.

My parents belonged to the rich set, although our house was shabby because we really didn't have the money. This didn't matter to the people of Concord, since my parents were their kind of people and fit in. My father came from a good southern family and played a mean Dixieland banjo and a decent game of tennis for someone with no form, and my mother was a Chittenden, which, if you know your blood, says worlds in itself. Her great-great-great-great-grandmother, Priscilla Chittenden, was the first woman to step on Plymouth Rock. The big thing in my family is getting on that rock first, though I don't know what we've done since except write long books about our breeding and marry each other and produce manic-depressives.

We lived in a Victorian house on Maple Street that had train tracks in the back and a side yard that was mostly dirt. We had margarine except on Sunday and did not have a house on the Cape, as did most of my parents' friends, driving instead, during my father's two-week summer vacation, fourteen hours to my grandmother's in Virginia, for my mother to be informed on a daily basis that television was ruining our eyes. All of us, except George, went to public school. George went to boarding school at age fourteen after breaking my father's 78 RPM recording of "Hummingbird, Hummingbird" over Harry's head.

George was the oldest, but Harry had always been first in my father's heart, due to the fact that George was born during the war and didn't meet our father until he was two, a rival

5

wrapped around our mother's leg. Also, while George had struggled with classical piano, Harry had played Dixieland clarinet like a professional by age ten.

"George is my favorite brother," I'd been fond of flinging in the faces of Spencer and Harry, as if this would wither them on the spot. George had fought like crazy with Harry—even in his teens, we'd had to allow an extra hour when we drove down to visit my grandmother for George to get out of the car in a huff and run away—but George was the only brother who never hit me, even on the day he had to drive me to horseback riding lessons, which I'd been taking at Miss Harrion's for three years straight.

"Left or right?" George had asked when we got to the end of our driveway.

"I dunno," I'd said.

George had always been nice to me. He would come home from boarding school and I would sit next to him when he played the piano, because nobody else would, and wait for him to miss that chord. George had known everything there was to know about popular music ("Does your chewing gum lose its flavor on the bedpost overnight, does your mother say don't chew it, and you swallow it in spite? Do you catch it on your tonsils and heave it left and right," boom, boom—he'd allow me to listen with him, sitting on the couch in the playroom), and whenever Spencer and I would fight, Spencer's biggest threat was if you don't do such and such, I'll tell George you don't like rock 'n' roll. No! No! I would cry, anything but that. Everything was nice when it was just George and me—George would even pretend not to notice when you sat there watching TV with Kleenex stuffed in your undershirt—but then Harry would always show up, and the next thing you knew there would be screaming and swearing and I would run to my room and pray and pray for their souls.

But George had never been home much, and it was Spencer, who was three years older than I, who had been my closest brother growing up. Spencer had what my father called "that pixielike quality" that made everyone who met him yearn for his arm around his shoulder, including those two eight-year-old girls Spencer, on his seventh birthday, had sat nestled between at *The King and I*, his arms resting comfortably over the backs of their chairs. George had liked rock 'n' roll in a musical way, but what Spencer had liked was to slick his hair back and stand in front of the mirror lip-synching the words to "Venus, If You Will," while fat Frannie Dangle and I, unsolicited, posed in the background as Venus and the little girl for Frankie Avalon, or Spencer, to thrill.

Early on Spencer had dropped out of the competition between Harry and George. When my father had had to call a family conference on the subject of Harry reading George's *Archie* and *Veronica* comic books but refusing to chip in to buy them and it was finally decided that Harry would have to rent them if he wanted to read them, Spencer's solution was to take a large stack of George's comics down to Mandy Viles, who was lying at death's door with scarlet fever. "Why, Spencer," Mrs. Viles had said at the door, choked with emotion, "how thoughtful," and then Spencer had charged her ninety-five cents.

Then of course there were the stories about how Spencer had taken care of me right after I was born and Mother was in the hospital all those months, with Spencer telling everyone I was his baby and riding me all over town on the back of his tricycle, although how he did this with a newborn I do not know, and how even when Mother came home two years later, when he was five, he had insisted that I sleep in his room. My mother's theory about Spencer's and my eventual falling-out (when he was eight and I was five) was that I never forgave him when he started having girlfriends, which he began, with easy success, very early on (Kitty Killebrew next door traveled first to George, then Harry, but it was finally Spencer, we noticed, who got her to pee into a milk bottle), and I must say I wasn't exactly wild about that Judy Ryan who sat next to me every Little League game to talk about Spencer. I loved going to watch Spencer play baseball because it meant I got to eat a Loretta Veal Parmigiana TV Dinner along with him before the game, instead of the three plain mounds of meat, green vegetable, and potato or rice the mothers of Concord served their families at each supper ("How does your mother do it?" my father would ask in wonder every night) followed, on our table, by the inevitable bowl of Del Monte Fruit Cocktail. My mother didn't believe it was healthy for us to have a lot of brownies or homemade cookies around the house, but the New, Improved Loretta Veal Parmigiana TV Dinner had a ground-breaking compartment, with a little square of apple pie in it that heated up right along with everything else.

Anyway, although Spencer's life had consisted of keeping the peace among a dozen little girls, in the end it had been me he needed to go to the bathroom next to the train tracks for his fourth-grade friends, or be the one who would buy his Halloween candy, beautifully stored in shiny mayonnaise jars weeks after I'd gobbled mine down, at a penny per candy corn. For better or worse, I was linked to Spencer, but it was Harry who had always been my idol.

"My brother Harry is handsome and plays clarinet," I'd informed the milk line in first grade. "Who cares?" had said Sandy Spaddorow. Harry was five years older than I and A plus straight through high school and captain of the debating team and lead in the play, and on his bedroom door had been a sign that said Knock Before Entering. When he'd allowed you into his immaculate room, you'd find him sitting at his desk with all the pens and pencils neatly lined up in rows, impatiently tapping his foot. Harry had wanted to be a doctor and he'd taken seven courses instead of four and in his spare time he had lifted Wendy Andrews's guinea pigs from their shallow graves as they died like clockwork one by one and dissected them in the basement while everyone in the neighborhood watched in open-mouthed awe. We were all good at going to school but Harry had been the genius, although the parents said they paid no truck to geniuses. When the school

8

had called to say a test had said that Harry was extremely gifted, my mother had replied that that was all very well, but it was no excuse for putting the carton of milk back in the icebox with just one drop of milk left in it because you were too lazy to throw it away. My mother believed in treating people as if they were normal even if they were not.

The Concord schools were keen on math and science—if you were in the Honor Division, your whole life was geared to calculus, which you began in ninth grade—and every year they had high school science fairs. I was nine the first time we all trooped up to see Harry compete. It was 1960, a big year for the United States trying like crazy to beat the Russians in technology, and the town had just built a brand-new, modernesque high school, with a low, flat tar-paper roof and mirrors instead of windows, on top of the old dump. The fair was held in the all-glass cafeteria, but it took us a while to find it, what with all the mirrors to bump into and my father's refusing to ask directions, and when we finally got there, it was hard to see anything, the glare was so bad. All the kids had fancy papier-mâché models of mountains erupting or huge digestive systems with epiglottises closing like gates over esophagi that their fathers had helped them make—even when we'd gone to him with our homework, my father had just shaken his head and wondered aloud how he got such smart kids. And there, far out of the way over in a corner, stood Harry, a freshman, with a couple of sticks glued together under a poster that said, Congruent Polygons in black, not even colored! Magic Marker, no cute little symbols or pictures or buttons to push, no nothing, arguing like mad with a couple of judges. I was so ashamed I wanted to die, but then of course Harry won first prize and went on to win the National Science Award. He entered those damn congruent polygons every year, and won every year until he graduated, and then we went to one more high school science fair to see Spencer win Third Prize for Effort for his attractive illustration of binary numbers ("Too much for me!" my father replied when Spencer started to explain his exhibit, which, basically, was just a set of light switches you turned on and off), after which our scientific curiosity as a family petered out.

I was absolutely terrified of Harry when I was little, and spoke to him only on rare occasions. Harry was a fourth-grade cross-guard monitor when I was in kindergarten, and once I got up my nerve to ask him if he would please turn the line around the next day. Monitors were allowed to turn the bus lines around so that the kids at the end of the line got to be at the beginning, the theory being it would teach the prompt, aggressive kids some kind of lesson, although what I cannot imagine. Anyway, the next day I carefully took my place at the end of the line, viewing my compatriots with pity, but Harry never swung it around. Later, when I asked him why, he yelled that he forgot, all right? and I spent the rest of the afternoon standing in front of the mirror trying to get my lips to turn upward so I wouldn't cry.

It was several years before I dared broach Harry again. Then one afternoon when I was about eleven I went into the kitchen and found him at the table eating bowls of cereal. Harry was growing ferociously in high school, hitting six-foot-seven by age fifteen (his junior year, since he had skipped a grade), and he would come home from school and eat boxes of cereal and jars of baby food, and still stay skinny as a rail. That day he was reading *Scientific American* and didn't seem to notice when I walked in.

"What's a virgin?" I burst out conversationally. Harry looked up with contempt and then went back to his reading.

"A virgin is someone who hasn't been laid," he finally said, turning a page. I stood quietly for a moment.

"What's 'laid' mean?" I asked.

"Jesus Christ," said Harry, and, throwing his magazine down, he left the room.

Looking back, I suppose Harry had been too perfect. In those days it was before you had shrinks on the radio so you didn't know much. Harry explained later that he'd been unhappy all that time he was the star, but it looked pretty good to me. He won half the awards at his high school graduation, and I will never forget that day as long as I live. My grandmother had come up for it, and the day before she had taken me down to Kussins and bought me a very expensive yellow dress with short, starched sleeves and two tucks in the bodice that let you stick out without anything there. "Why, thank you, Mother," my mother had said when she saw it, tears in her eyes, although it turned out my grandmother had charged the dress to my father.

The graduation ceremony was on the football field and we sat high up in the bleachers: my grandmother with her extravagant good posture ("Hitch your bosom to a star," she'd sung out to her three daughters) and her leopard hat from the Sears catalog, from which she ordered all her clothes even though she was rich as Croesus; my parents and George and Spencer and me; and my Great-Aunt Elizabeth, who wintered on Beacon Street in Boston and did not believe it was ever necessary to say disagreeable things.

I don't know how the other families felt sitting up there in those rickety stands, but our family certainly wasn't bored as award after award was presented to Harry. "To someone we can really look up to," said Mr. Cataloni, the principal, and how we chuckled at the fine joke as he craned his neck toward Harry and handed him the most prestigious honor of all, the American Flag Award, which, upon returning to his seat, Harry casually tossed to the ground, dampening our spirits a hair and causing my father to look to the heavens for strength. It was a long ceremony, and yet we found we were not weary when it came time for the valedictory speech, by Harry, all about how the post office was really socialistic, when you thought about it, so don't tell him socialism was so bad. This was a daring speech for Concord in 1963 and brought in not a few fuming letters to the *Concord Journal*. On the other hand, my Great-Aunt Elizabeth, who was very conservative and had her doubts about the paternity of Jackie Kennedy's baby, thought it a lovely speech about the mails, and my grandmother commented that Harry had a fine patrician voice, like all the Bulkeleys'. Our hearts were full the day Harry graduated from high school. Then, that fall, he was off to Harvard.

We drove him down to Cambridge one Sunday in mid-September. I sat in the back with Harry, who paid me no attention, and imagined how I would look in a pair of the new knee-high leather boots that you took your shoes off to put on. George was back at college; he had picked Princeton, my father's alma mater, in his unceasing efforts to please him—there were many, many years to go before George, his table manners casually corrected one day by my father, would respond, "You've resented me since the day I was born!" I don't know where Spencer was—probably off with some girl. When Spencer had arrived as a freshman at the high school in Harry's senior year, so dapper, his curly hair the envy of my mother's friends, all the senior girls had thought he was cute as a bug. "Hi, Spencer-baby," they would call out when they passed him in the halls. Spencer had a relaxed, appreciative way with girls, which he got directly from my father, who, once when he saw Joan Fontaine hurrying along a street, tipped his hat and said, "Good morning, Miss Fontaine," stopping her dead in her tracks and beginning a lifelong friendship.

We were all pretty excited that day. The parents were dressed up and Harry was in his new madras jacket. I was wearing a dark-green wool wraparound skirt, a green-and-white tiny-print blouse, and a green wool cardigan with the required bottom three buttons buttoned up, though it must have been ninety degrees. My mother bought me two new outfits for fall every year and I wore them beginning the first day of school come hell or high water. I was also sporting my blue wing-tip glasses with the sparkles, which Spencer said made me look like the new Buick.

We took Harry over to his dorm and met his roommates, and you could tell Harry wanted us to leave but all the parents kept standing around looking proud and trying to get in a brag or two about their sons. The whole time my mind was on this science test I had the next day. I wasn't too good at science—they'd lost me when they'd said, "Look at this desk top and realize there are millions of atoms whirling around in there"—and I looked out the window at Harvard yard, with the parents and sons walking around with suitcases and the late afternoon sun hitting the fall leaves, and I got a lump in my throat that didn't go away until later that night, when I happened to see part of *Dumbo* on "Walt Disney." I had thought it was time for "Twentieth Century" when I'd turned on the set, and then the next thing I knew Spencer caught me crying at the part where Dumbo's mother sticks her trunk out of the circus car she's locked up in and rocks Dumbo, but fortunately I didn't care.

I was in seventh grade the year Harry went to Harvard and, for me at least, no year had ever been better. It was the first and only time I ever achieved a mass popularity. Even "the cheapies," who had split from the rest of us on the issue of make-out parties, liked me because you couldn't tell I was a brain. I became the first girl ever to be elected to the Student Council who was also in the Honor Division, on account of making a speech that made fun of all the usual candidate speeches about how you promised to serve the class to the best of your ability, which did not endear me to Mr. Hamm, who took the Student Council and its duties of deciding whether to have Coke or ginger ale at the sock hops very seriously and had once, three years before, slammed Spencer up against a row of lockers after a basketball game because, although Spencer had scored well, he hadn't shown the proper spirit. It was suspected at the time that Mr. Hamm's feelings about Spencer had been colored by the petition Spencer had presented, written painstakingly with legalese supplied by Harry, in which the student body hereby had requested forthwith the right to do the twist at the eighth-grade prom. "I'll have your head for this!" Mr. Hamm had roared.

13

My brash self-confidence won me the lead in the seventh-grade play (even though the lead wasn't so great, in that I had to play Rip Van Winkle in full white beard), as it always had won me the lead, every year from the third grade, when I was awarded the role of the Revolutionary wife in *No Braver Soldier*, a patriotic play of no apparent plot, where I got to say the daringly romantic line (after the dashing, popular Wade O'Sullivan had said, "God bless thee") "And thee, Lubin," to the sixth grade, when I portrayed the princess in *The Proud Princess*, during which the entire auditorium fell to a trembling hush as Wade O'Sullivan, ennobled now (though wearing, for some reason, a ridiculous, though authentic, jeweled turban cupped over his head), lifted my hand to his mouth and carefully kissed his own thumb. Whether it was my talent or my belief in my talent that landed these roles I will never know. But whatever it was, it was still with me that year, not to flee till the next, when forever more at every audition I would find my tongue lying like a lump of wet clay at the bottom of my mouth.

But in the fall of seventh grade I still believed I was beautiful, a brave conclusion, based as it was upon the blindness of a father's devotion and my own literal blindness, as I squinted into the mirror without my glasses at a pleasant blur of pinks and tans. So strong was this conviction that I had two boyfriends, with whom I had been going for two years. Every grade since I could remember I had had a boyfriend, though none of them had ever been aware of it until Warren Billings, whose stepfather was making him go to private school with all the snobs, and Chickie Lombardo, who clucked in class and got away with it because he was already a hood. Warren was the main boyfriend—I'd started up with him in fifth grade, after he'd thrown chewed-up erasers at me on the school bus. Warren had come right up to me the next morning and asked me to go bowling, but I hadn't been able to because of a hair appointment, which, it was felt by my mother, it was important to stick to. Before, I'd just gone along with the brothers

14

to the barbershop, but this appointment was in Boston at a real hairdresser's. Warren must have admired my Yankee tenacity because, though he took Joanie Stevenson bowling that Saturday, he stopped by to see me every day after. It got so that each afternoon I could be found out in the driveway shooting baskets and looking down the street.

"Waiting for Warren Billings?" Spencer would call out derisively from the window, which hotly I would deny, and then Warren, and later Chickie, who joined up kind of free lance that first spring, would happen by on their bikes. I would stand there at the edge of our driveway, with its broken-up pieces of asphalt, talking, and letting the merest bit of my undershirt strap show, hoping, against logic, it would be construed to be a bra. Sometimes we would bike over to Walden Pond, or in the winter go ice-skating on the Concord River, which, one snowless year after the marshes had flooded, allowed us to skate all over town every day after school until the sky turned red. Mostly I skated on my ankles, but Warren and Chickie didn't seem to mind, and they both gave me silver dog pins that I wore on my lapel like medals.

Chickie Lombardo eventually fell away to the crowd that was wearing frosted lipstick and padded bras, but the March I was in seventh grade, Warren took me to the Groton School dance. I was staying at Frannie Dangle's that night, on account of my parents' being away to be with my grandmother when she died, and Warren and his stepfather picked me up there in their charcoal-gray Rambler. I was wearing a baby-blue polished cotton dress with an overjacket that was supposed to stop at the waist but made it only halfway down my front, and Warren was in a suit, with his hair slicked behind his ears. I sat in the backseat with him, feeling suddenly like I needed to wash my face, while Warren's stepfather, a large, handsome man with a flat-top, drove us in silence to the school.

"How come you're never around anymore?" Warren asked when we got out on the dance floor, referring to the fact that since the winter I was never out shooting baskets but eating brownie batter over at Sukie Mears's.

"I got stuff to do," I'd said, unable to impart greater meaning to the recent inclination I had had to plop my lumpening body safely in the kitchens of other girls. We'd shuffled around the dance floor aimlessly for a while, for despite all those years of learning the fox-trot and the cha-cha-cha, and, as a special treat, the polka ("The twist! The twist!" we had shouted to the deaf ears of Miss Dredge, our dancing instructor), I have never once used a step of any legitimate dance in real life. The only other public school girl there was Betsy Ryerson, a popular eighth-grader who looked cute even with the elastics of her braces snapping. She and Bruce Sinclair had waltzed around the room cheek to cheek.

"We could dance like that," Warren had said in a gruff voice, and, as it turned out, he was right, although, as Warren was shorter, it was more like neck to cheek. We'd danced close in silence until the last number, half of Warren's clammy face adhering to my neck, our bodies rigidly stuck together as we moved one inch forward and one inch back, crossing the line to sin.

"See Sally Ames over there?," Warren had finally asked, "Her father's really rich." Then the lights had gone up and we'd moved awkwardly to the swarming foyer, careful not to bump up against each other as we fished for our coats, the large form of Warren's stepfather looming beyond in the open doorway.

"Night," I'd said casually to Warren on the Dangles' front porch, as if I danced close every day of the week, and then I'd opened the door to Mrs. Dangle, who told me my grandmother had just died. My grandmother hated little children and never paid any attention to you until you were twelve and your parents couldn't stand you, and then down you'd go for the summer to her big, romantic stone house overlooking the Shenandoah, on the farm that lost money every year, and she'd sit up with you till all hours drinking from her pitcher of gin.

16

"Dahling, would you like some lemonade?" she'd slurred to me one bleary night, motioning to the pitcher. "Oh no, thank you!" I'd sung out, thrilled to find my suspicions as to the contents of the pitcher unfounded, yet mysteriously not thirsty.

Anyway, my grandmother's dying didn't seem to affect me too much, except that we inherited enough to send me to tennis camp the following summer—though not enough to stop Warren Billings from taking Sally Ames to the next Groton School dance. It took them a while to find my grandmother's money, which had been hidden in thirty-four banks all around the country because she didn't want anyone to know how much she had. "I don't want anyone to love me for my money," she had always said, and, in truth, as I opened my Christmas present of seven plastic pens that didn't write, with my name misspelled in gold ink, bought from the back of a cereal box, I did not. "All I know," my mother said later, "is that all our troubles started *after* we inherited Mother's money," but of course she was wrong. Now we could have butter instead of margarine, and that summer I got to go to a rich kids' camp instead of a church camp, where you had to pray every morning and you didn't even sleep in cabins, just tents on platforms, and you only went swimming in the early morning when it was freezing—when it was midday and hot as can be you were stuck in some stuffy cabin making pot holders. At Powhatan Tennis Camp, for a thousand bucks a month, I was allowed to sit around with a couple of girls and eat too much. That summer was the only summer in my life I wasn't interested in boys, though if you look at pictures of me, with a terrible pixie haircut sticking out of a nylon headband and the sun glaring off my sparkly glasses, it was probably just as well.

The point is, I was so happy—and then one morning, Harry woke up in Bugs Bunny's body and didn't dare look in the mirror until he was sure he had his own body back again.

The parents must have told me Harry had had a breakdown, but all I keep remembering is Harry coming home for Sunday dinners morose that fall, his sophomore year, and not saying one word the whole meal and afterward going with the parents into the living room and closing the sliding mahogany doors. And then, he didn't come home for Christmas.

The truth is, I didn't ask any questions. I was thirteen and I couldn't fit what had happened to Harry into a brain whirring with the life-and-death concerns of buying a girdle I didn't need or coercing my hair to curl out instead of under, or whatever it is that is so consuming when you're adolescent. So I didn't think about Harry, until one Sunday afternoon during George's spring vacation, when George, Spencer, and the parents went off to see *Tom Jones* on the proceeds from the swear box. I'd instituted the swear box a few years before and it had done rather well for itself, until the day my father'd cut his hand on the electric carving knife.

"Goddam it to hell," he had cried, as the blood dripped into the kitchen sink.

"One nickel, please," I'd returned.

"That's it!" my father had said and run upstairs to crack open the swear box. I refused to go with them to *Tom Jones,* in which, to my knowledge, the actresses wore low-cut dresses, on the grounds that the swear-box money should be donated to the church.

So I was home alone that Sunday, and I pulled down the shades in the living room and turned on the lights so it would seem cozy, even though it was a beautiful, sunny spring day, and got out a couple of old dolls. I still played dolls now and then, but it wasn't working so well anymore, which, at my advanced age, one would think not. A lot of things weren't working so well anymore in the eighth grade. The year before I had thought I was Queen of the May, but in the fall of eighth grade I got my first pair of contact lenses. You had to wait until you were thirteen to get contact lenses and then you had to go once a week for a month to take contact lens lessons from this blue-eyelidded woman who would demonstrate with coy little winks how contacts would allow you to flirt with your eyes, and then you'd go home and be sure a contact lens, lost in your eye, was headed directly for your brain.

"You know," Spencer had said, when he'd got a look at my new winkable eyes, "maybe you're the type who looks better in glasses."

At any rate, I was playing dolls so late in life I was acting out story lines from movies like *Spartacus* and *Ben-Hur,* to the exhaustion of one Dutch boy doll of dubious gender who had to play all the male parts, only catching his breath when the sex scenes came. When the sex scenes came, I simply placed him on top of an appropriate female doll, as if I were putting toast in the toaster, and left the room until they were done. I was not terribly fond of the fact of sex, but, once over the initial horror, I had adopted a businesslike attitude toward it, calmly working out a theory that the parents were doing it whenever I could see the red light of their electric blanket in the darkness of their bedroom.

I had been playing for an hour or so, but it hadn't been much fun, and I was kind of wandering around, wondering what to do next, when the phone rang. It was Harry, and he didn't even say hello, just "Tell the parents to get me a lawyer. I've got to get out of here," all in one breath, and then he hung up before I could answer. For some reason I thought he had gotten a girl in trouble, even though it didn't go with what he had said. In those days getting a girl in trouble was the big thing, the worst thing that could happen, and I began to worry about Harry and the consequence of his sin so much I couldn't continue with my dolls, so I put them away and went up to sit in the attic, where my father had a box of John O'Hara paperbacks. The thing about John O'Hara novels was that they always had this girl on the cover smoking a cigarette, wearing only a slip, but then you'd read the whole book and if you were lucky you'd get "and they closed the bedroom door." Anyway, I was going to tell Mother about Harry's call, but I forgot.

Chapter Two

It was when Harry came out of the hospital that September, so changed, and started coming home for Sunday dinners and leaving his wallet hanging around, with the blue plastic condom case peeking out, that the parents decided to send me away to school to get me away from the influence of my brothers—although really the only influence I was under was the influence of Betsy Ryerson. Cool as a cucumber, I ignored Harry and Spencer and their goings-on. All I wanted at age fourteen was to wear shirtwaist dresses and matching cardigans and have my hair work. Betsy Ryerson had the most perfect hair, a full bubble cut, each individual curl plopping gently into place, and I tried and tried to duplicate it, sleeping on my chin, motionless, my hair in giant pop-on wire rollers ("How's the reception tonight?" Spencer would ask) that popped off like clockwork in the middle of the night. "Plink, plink," I would hear, and know, without looking at the clock, that it was three A.M. Betsy Ryerson had gone away to school that fall, returning home for weekends sporting a gold class ring on her little finger, and suddenly I, too, yearned for an all-girls school where you didn't have to be feminine doing

21

math or wonder desperately, when you walked into class, how you were ever going to get to your chair without everyone looking at you.

At first my parents wanted me to go to Concord Academy, where the girls had long, beautiful hair and big bottoms, and every morning my mother would read to me from a collection of little speeches the headmistress had had privately published. "'Girls,'" I would hear just as I started my Grape-nuts, "'let's speak frankly about sex.'" Then it was decided that Concord Academy was not far away enough. This decision came down the Monday after Harry had followed my mother around the house singing, with great meaning, "The Times, They Are a-Changing," accompanying himself fiercely on his flute, or, rather, my flute. I had passed Harry my flute one day when he'd come in on me while I was practicing "Telemann in F Major" in lively competition with my metronome. Even George had refused to duet with me on account of my remarkable independence from the convention of keeping time. With a shrug, Harry had taken the instrument and played a jazz riff on it, though he had never touched the flute in his life.

"Do you want my flute, Harry?" I had asked, and that was that.

Another reason, probably, for this swerve away from Concord Academy on the part of my parents was that I was not, at that time, or, for that matter, for a long time thereafter, exactly what you would call a delight to have around, although to the outside world I was nice as pie. "Mrs. Owens says you are so polite and a joy to be with," the parents had remarked with a baffled air when they'd found me carving "I hate Mother" with a safety pin on my bedroom door.

In the end, I picked the Greenfield School for Girls over the Willow Farm School, where the headmaster slid down the banister to meet us and the kids lived in horse stalls, because I liked the rooms better. I was accepted that winter and all set to enroll the following fall for sophomore year. But then, that spring, everything changed.

22

It was 1966, the last year guys you barely knew called you up and asked you out on dates. I hadn't technically been out on a date since the Groton School dance, but I had developed crushes on a couple of seniors in Spencer's class, and would walk way out of my way between class periods, my heart racing with anticipation, just to pass Jeff Sonnenfeld or Pony Raker in the hall. "Hi," they might or might not say, depending upon whether they noticed me. I got the best view of my crushes every Friday night at the Catacombs, the coffeehouse Spencer had started in our musty cellar, in the room in which we were going to build a fallout shelter in 1961 and lie on the floor while the bombs fell, eating beans out of a can and shooting the neighbors as they rushed to break their way in. Spencer played guitar at these subterranean affairs, sitting on an inverted garbage can, and tried to make his lovely, sweet voice sound raspy and nasal. "The answer, my friend, is blowing in the wind," he would bleat out while Harry backed him up on flute, or saxophone, or washtub bass. In his earlier years Spencer had flailed about, trying different instruments, and finally discovered folk music, flirting briefly with the banjo and the clean-cut music of the Kingston Trio before finding a home in the guitar and the angry songs of Bob Dylan. Four years before, when Spencer was only thirteen, he had heard that Dylan was coming to play at Club 47 in Cambridge, and so had written him a nice letter, figuring that "Bob" might not care for motels and offering him a place to stay at our house. At any rate, it was at the Catacombs that Spencer and Harry first started playing together. Harry had never deigned to play music with Spencer before his breakdown, but when he'd come out of the hospital, raging at the parents but shaky inside, it was Spencer who had taken him under his wing.

As for me, I was allowed the privilege of selling Dixie cups of Hawaiian Punch to the high school students who gathered at the Catacombs, looking not exactly like Joan Baez in my Peter Pan collars and lumpy hairdo, struck dumb by the beauty of each and every one of Spencer's friends. One time

Pony Raker, a serious, stocky boy whose father's name was Horse, left his army surplus jacket behind and I donned it, still holding Pony's shape, and walked around in it for hours.

It wasn't until June that a couple of Spencer's friends finally asked me out, and when they drove me to the movies I was careful to sit halfway between them and the car door. Spencer had told me that if you sat clinging to the door it looked like you didn't like the guy, and if you sat right up next to him, it made you look fast. I did a bit of kissing on these dates, but I do not believe I ever spoke a single sentence because Spencer had also advised me that he did not like girls who talked. There were many rules that Spencer patiently explained to me. Spencer was always very paternal, which I think was one of the keys to his phenomenal success with women. Even when we were little and Spencer had played doctor with all my friends, he had had the perfect air, all business, very clinical, yet somehow caring. (It was with a concerned but careful not-to-alarm air that Spencer had quietly informed Mother one day that I was lacking a babyhole.) You listened to Spencer in matters of romance because in this field he was very brilliant. He never even had to take a new date out to the movies: he would just invite the girl over and build a fire in the fireplace in the living room. They would sit in silence for a while, reflecting, and then Spencer would say, softly, "Ever notice how no two flames are ever the same height?" count to three, then gently place his arm over her shoulders.

Then in August I met Robert Whipler. Robert Whipler was a junior in high school and the assistant golf pro at the country club that summer. I always felt a little out of place at the club, because most of the kids who hung around there went to private school, and one day I was standing around by myself in a pair of beige Lanz shorts when Robert Whipler came over and started talking to me. Robert was very masculine and handsome and wore Canoe aftershave. We talked and talked those first few days, sitting cross-legged on the floor of the pro shop, and I figured we were just friends until we took a bus into Harvard Square and Robert kissed me right in the middle of some Jean-Paul Belmondo movie, his gum miraculously disappearing, only to surface again after the kiss. Afterward we went over to the Wursthaus, where they served us each a beer, and then we walked over to Harvard Yard and lay on the grass in front of Widener Library and made out alongside the Harvard and Radcliffe students who were doing the same.

"It's just like we were going to Harvard," said Robert, after which we took the bus to Robert's house and he showed me childhood photographs, and told me I had great legs, which I knew wasn't true because Spencer and Harry had told me I had legs just like Mother's.

I spent every day, all day, with Robert Whipler, hanging around the pro shop listening to "Sunny . . . Sunny . . ." on the radio or, more poignantly, "Will I see you in September, or lose you to a summer love?" which didn't exactly fit the situation of me going away to school, but, in the general spirit of the thing, came close enough.

"That's not going to happen to us, lambie," Robert would vow, "no way." Then, during lunch or after the last golf lesson, we would go across the street to a field nobody seemed to own and lie looking up at the brilliant sky and kissing, surrounded by broken bottles glistening in the sun.

One night, about two weeks into the relationship, I brought Robert home to have dinner with the parents. Robert was very polite and chatted amiably with my mother and father, who were always very nice to everyone. Most parents are critical of their children's boyfriends and girlfriends, but ours always acted grateful toward whomever we brought home, as if they were thanking their lucky stars that anyone was interested. During the meal my mother might well have interviewed Robert "as a member of the younger generation," as this was at the beginning of her intellectual period, but I cannot say, because the entire time I was convulsed by giggles. "And where do you live, Robert?" my mother would ask sincerely, and I would laugh and laugh until the tears streamed down my face.

When dinner was over Robert and I went out to the barn we had instead of a garage, and upstairs to this kind of apartment Spencer had set up with an old couch and a stereo and red lighting, and made out for a while. "I love you," said Robert amidst the thrashing, which meant, according to Spencer, that I was to take my shirt off ("But never, under *any circumstances*, anything below"). Afterward we went outside, where it was cooler, and sat on the redwood chairs under the apple tree, Robert's cigarette end an orange dot in the middle of black.

"Did you hear what I said, baby?" Robert asked, as the dot moved upward. "I said that I love you. Do you know what that means?"

"Oh yes," I answered. If anyone knew what it meant it was I, as I buttoned up my flower-print blouse. "I know . . . I mean, I'm glad," I stammered and then I knew he was waiting for something more and I was grateful that it was pitch dark. "I mean, you know, same with me," I managed to get out without much grace.

But I wasn't sure and I couldn't bring myself to say the words, though there were moments, in the aftermath of our dark embraces, when I came near. I would turn to Robert with a full heart, my eyes smarting in the sudden clicked-on light, and there he would be smiling away at me, vigorously snapping his gum, which always jinxed the deal. I don't know whether I was too self-conscious, or too uncertain, or too burdened with the importance of it all (I'd never in my life told anyone I'd loved them, not even the members of my family) to declare myself, but it didn't seem to matter. With Robert I was happier than ever I had been before.

The romance had been going on for less than a month when off I went to Greenfield, driving the whole way up to the Berkshires with the parents, punishing them with a pregnant silence. I no longer wanted to leave; for days I had begged and begged them not to make me, not now when I finally could walk the hallways of high school proudly, linked to my handsome, wisecracking boyfriend. Why should I go to Greenfield when it would ruin my life?

"You must learn that when you make a decision, you must stick to it" had been my mother's answer.

"But what about Robert Whipler?" I had cried.

"If Robert cares for you, he will still care for you when you are away at school," she had replied, forgetting we were very young. Even Spencer, who was off to Oberlin College that September, had sided with me, but it was no use arguing when there was principle involved.

The day before I left, Robert took me into Harvard Square and bought me a real ring at a jeweler's, and then we went and sat on a bench overlooking the Charles River.

"Maybe one day we'll get married," he said, putting his arm around me. "Who knows."

"Who knows," I agreed.

"I love you, and don't you ever forget it," Robert Whipler said, and certainly I never have.

My parents were as miserable as I, as we drove up to Greenfield, my father wearing a puzzled expression and my mother the set look you always saw on her lips in church when the minister talked about being selfish. When we arrived at my assigned dorm, girls were running around with their parents and trunks of clothes, being all happy to see one another.

"There's a pretty girl," my father said, watching someone named Jacquie, who was gabbing away on the dorm phone, and the next thing you knew he'd struck up a conversation with her about how she was from Chicago. I remained true to myself and spoke to the parents only when absolutely necessary.

"Where do you want your trunk?" my father asked when we got to my room.

"I couldn't care less," I said. My mother unpacked my clothes while I slumped glumly on the bed.

"Well," the parents said, hovering anxiously in the middle of the room, "good-bye, darling. Have a good time. We love you." And they kissed me as I sat straight as a ramrod.

Robert wrote me every day that first week—I love you, I love you, I love you, 'round and 'round in a circle—but I still wasn't sure if I really loved him back, until he called me the second week to say he was going with lanky Deb Soblosky, who was two years older and went to Catholic school, because she went farther. Well, I thought tragically, at least I have the ring, although even that was not to be the case. A letter arrived that week asking me if I would please send it back, which I did, and really it was the only thing I ever blamed Robert Whipler for.

You didn't have to give a whole lot of thought about what you were going to do next at the Greenfield School for Girls, because every second was planned, from the forty-five minutes when you prayed in the morning to the fifteen minutes at the end of the day, called "Happy Time" on the schedule, when you laughingly washed your face. The big treat was the one day a year when the headmistress appeared on the lawn wearing a little peaked hat and called out, "To the mountains!" at which point all activities were daringly tossed to the winds and, instead of going to classes, you got to trudge up cliffs, singing jolly songs.

I was used to living with all boys, and at Greenfield it was all girls, with high, shrill voices, who begged one another to make them stay on diets and then, when they were caught with an entire box of chocolate-chip cookies, shouted out, "I hate you! I hate you!" All my life I had dreamed of sitting around in ruffly underwear giggling femininely with a bunch of friends while putting on toenail polish, but at Greenfield I arose in the morning with a clutching at my throat and went heavily through the required activities—chapel, classes, field hockey on the breathtaking lawns—as if every member of my family had been gunned down in the streets the day before.

Daily I pleaded over the phone with the parents to let me come home, but even after I threw up for them on Parents Weekend they were very big on me sticking it out.

"This will help you later in life," my mother would say as if my life were to consist of going to stodgy boarding schools. "You will thank me for this." Even George, who had been miserably homesick at his own boarding school, down South, but had never been given the option of coming home, wrote me a long letter about "sticking it out," but it was no use. Finally, at the school's suggestion, I was sent down to a fancy psychiatrist in Cambridge, who spent much of our hour video-taping me sitting in his office. I told him all about how I was getting A pluses at Greenfield because the public school in Concord was really better and how I hated the structured days and being in classes with all girls.

"Lizzie wants to be home to share in her brothers' suffering," the psychiatrist told my mother, and that was that. My mother was a great believer in the experts.

It was a beautiful October day the afternoon my father picked me up to bring me home from Greenfield, and I remember him driving past the orange and yellow trees, sighing and sighing and saying he just didn't understand why I hadn't been happy. He had this image of me, popular and pink-cheeked, sitting at some football game surrounded by open-faced boys with names like Ned and Bill. To my father popularity was the big thing—when Sharon Gap got pregnant freshman year he had asked what was the matter, hadn't she been popular—and if you didn't get a lot of phone calls and boys coming to the door, you always thought you had let him down. I felt bad for my father, but still it was a nice drive. I was so incredibly glad to be going home.

Slouched on the back porch to greet me was Spencer, who had left for Oberlin two weeks after I'd left for Greenfield and had returned home two weeks before me. He had slumped around the campus smoking marijuana, taking all his cuts for the semester in his first week, until one day, as Spencer himself

29

had told me over the phone, he had drifted into the dean's office. "I think it's time for me to go," Spencer had said, and evidently the dean had not disagreed. When my father received a message at work the following day to call operator 46 in Oberlin, Ohio, somehow he had suspected it was not good news and his heart had sunk. Years before, my mother had hidden away a secret piece of paper on which she had forecast that Spencer would become a pediatrician when he grew up, but, in truth, hopes for Spencer's higher education had been on the wane since his high school graduation, which the parents had had to force him to attend. "Thanks, baby," Spencer had said straight into the microphone when the ancient Miss Klipinger had handed him his diploma.

"Why didn't you stop him?" my father said over the phone to the Oberlin dean, who mumbled something to the effect that really, it wasn't the sort of circumstance they had had experience in, obviously taken aback by the whole affair, and it was a week before the parents even knew where Spencer was.

"If you don't come up here now, we're coming down to find you," the parents threatened when Spencer happened to call in from some pay phone in South Carolina. Spencer told me later that the first thing he heard as he stepped foggily and miserably off the plane in Boston was his name being paged crisply all over the airport: "Spencer Reade, please report to the blue information desk, Spencer Reade, . . ." the parents panicking when he hadn't been the first person out the door. He'd been thinking the whole flight back that as soon as he got home he was going straight out to get a job, but when my father, as they were driving back to Concord, turned around to Spencer, huddled in the backseat of the car between his guitar and laundry bags of clothes, and said, "The first thing you're going to do tomorrow morning is get a job," Spencer thought to himself, *No, no, I do not think I will be doing that.*

30

I walked up the steps to the back porch that sunny October afternoon when it was my turn to crawl back home, and Spencer put his arm around me.

"The family failures," he said, and we walked into the playroom together.

The next day, Harry came out to dinner. He was sitting at the kitchen table alone when I first saw him.

"So, Harry," I said, "how's your sex life?" and instantly we were best friends.

Chapter Three

I returned to public school that November as a sophomore and started getting all B's, which in the Honor Division was like flunking out, on account of having become a deep person and recognizing the irrelevancy of life. I picked up some of this philosophy from Harry, calling in collect from the slums of Porter Square, but most of it I learned from Spencer, who at eighteen was now a day patient at Brookhill, the fancy mental hospital that was like an alma mater to my mother's family, where for thousands of dollars he played basketball. Spencer wasn't crazy like Harry, who'd had to sleep over. The parents gave Spencer the old Saab, and every morning he would drop me off at school on his way over to Brookhill, putting on his shoes and socks as he drove and sharing with me his most recent insights.

"I don't need money," he confided to me one day, and I was pretty impressed until we stopped at Anderson's and Spencer charged five ginger ales and two Sara Lee cakes to the parents, and then I told him he was just like Thoreau, who you knew had been getting his laundry done up at Emerson's while he lived in the woods. Personally, I had always hated

Thoreau; the writings of Louisa May Alcott, on the other hand, had had a profound influence on my life. My mother spoke of an excruciating period in which I called her Marmee and helped with the dishes every two seconds. My father was also a Concord author, I should mention. His books *Business-man's Banjo* and *You Can Play the Uke* can be found in the public library right up on the Concord Authors shelf, next to Emerson and Thoreau.

In addition to frozen cakes and ginger ale, Spencer also consumed chocolate pudding that year he prepped at Brook-hill, two bowls of which he made up every morning and put in the refrigerator to greet him when he got home after a hard day at the mental hospital. Once, as a joke, my father carefully scraped out the two bowls and placed them back in the icebox, and then got me to hide with him in the pantry to see Spencer's reaction. We watched Spencer enter the kitchen and with an uncharacteristically light step walk over to the refrigerator and open the door. In his face we saw his whole world crumble. "I've gone too far!" my father cried out, springing from the pantry. "It's a joke, nothing but a joke!" And in an instant he slammed the two full bowls he had carefully set aside into Spencer's hands.

Spencer and I were buddies now that we both had suffered. In the late afternoons we sat in the playroom together with the headphones on, listening to Bob Dylan sing about the shallowness of society and the pain of being. "Stuck inside of Mobile with the Memphis blues again," Dylan would warble and Spencer and I would puff our cigarettes and nod our heads, thinking, *How true.* I had tried smoking Camels but to save my soul I couldn't take a drag without the tobacco coming out all over my mouth, so I smoked Tareyton 100s, which still made me sick as a dog but, in a way, that was the point. Spencer had what he called a "message table" in the playroom, which held an open Bible on it and on top of that, an hour-glass, which was supposed to set the tone. I don't think even Spencer knew what it meant, but nobody dared ask. Spencer taught me how to be deep and depressed that fall, but he did it to be nice—I was pretty lonely at school after I came back from Greenfield. I'd already missed Mr. Downey's goldfish committing suicide, flinging itself out of the bowl and across the room during the filmstrip "Andrew Carnegie and the Robber Barons." Plus, when you'd been away at private school, people kind of thought you were snobby. One morning I'd walked into class and found "Go back to Greenfield" scrawled on my desk in Jonathan Seniger's handwriting.

"You may not be beautiful on the outside, Lizzie, but you're beautiful on the inside," Spencer told me, and at the time, it was the best I could get.

The year before, I had prayed to God that Spencer wasn't on drugs, but now I understood that the fact that he smoked marijuana meant that he was doing something important, although exactly what was unclear. Every night after the parents and I went to bed, Spencer would stay up watching Johnny Carson, lying on the playroom couch smoking pot and drinking cases of ginger ale as if it was a mission. Sometimes Harry would call in to watch the show with Spencer over the phone, and he and Spencer would toke up and then forty-five minutes might elapse before they'd even remember they were holding receivers to their ears.

Spencer would leave the playroom door wide open during these sessions and the sweet smoke would waft up to the parents' bedroom.

"I smell something funny," my mother would say, waking up with a jolt and sitting up in bed.

"You're just imagining things," my father would assure her half-asleep, praying against hope that that would be the end of it, but, as always, my mother would feel the matter needed further worrying, and after a little while they would get out of bed and I would hear them brushing their teeth over it in the bathroom that connected our rooms. Later it was "I'll try pot as soon as it's legal," but then the parents, though liberals, were pretty unhip about drugs.

35

"I bet he's smoking that LSD," my mother would say whenever she saw someone almost get hit by a car.

Saturdays I would go with Spencer to Brookhill to watch him in a basketball game—I don't know whom they played, I guess rival mental institutions. When Harry had been at Brookhill, two years before, he hadn't been playing any basketball that I knew about, but then I hadn't known much about anything because I'd never even visited him—though I must have known he was there because once my father had stopped by to see Harry on the way to take me out for my birthday lunch.

It was my fourteenth birthday, and for it I had already received a dachshund puppy just like the one that cavorted with the girl with the blond ponytail every month on the cover of *Calling All Girls.* I had begged and begged for years for this symbol of girlish happiness, but the parents had always maintained it wouldn't be fair to Scout, the mutt the neighbors had left behind when I was eight. Then, suddenly, it was almost as if they had become desperate to oblige, first presenting me with Sir Edward, a sweet miniature who pined away and died the first week because of a giant worm inside that nobody could do anything about, and then driving me over to the house of Mrs. De Leon, a woman with winged eyebrows who slept with seven pedigree dachshunds under her covers. We returned with a big yapping sausage of a dog, conceived, as we were graphically informed, of "good young sperm, not that crumbly old sperm you're getting these days if you aren't careful." Aphrodite I called her, due to the fact that whenever a male entered the room, she would roll her dense, cylindrical body over and expose her nipples.

Anyway, we always had a father-daughter lunch in Boston on my birthday, and that year my father took one of his short-cuts that always turn out to be long-cuts, probably thinking to himself, *We're going to Boston, why not zip by the hospital and cheer up Harry* (who probably had been staring at a speck of dirt on some wall for the last ten days) *with the latest ball scores?*

36

and the next thing I knew we were in Lincoln, driving up the elegant, curving driveway of Brookhill. It was a gray day in March, the sky one endless cloud, and I sat waiting for my father in the parking lot, drawing train tracks disappearing into the distance in the dust on the windshield of the car. It seemed like forever but it was probably only a few minutes before my father came out, giving me a wave as he puckered his lips into the whistle that was his second nature, and walked toward me with that brisk, no-nonsense way he'd had when he'd ushered at the Episcopal church.

We drove into Boston to eat at The Top of the Hub, which was on the sixty-fifth floor of the new Prudential Center and offered a view of the entire city when it wasn't socked in by clouds. Why we didn't change our reservations with the weather so bad I do not know, except that it is typical of my family, in which stick-to-itness runs in the blood. In the living-room bookshelves was an imposing but unthumbed volume entitled *Theodore Chittenden: His Life and Forebears,* written painstakingly, at nobody's request, by my great-grandfather, chronicling nothing (in one chapter the family moves from Boston to Georgia, and in the next they move back), in which can be gleaned that not a few of my ancestors were Tories in the Revolution, sticking fast to Mother England and, at the first crack of gunfire, fleeing quick as bunnies to Canada to safeguard their principles.

We had lobster Newburg, meager bits of lobster with Campbell's soup poured over the top, not unlike what the matrons of Concord were fond of whipping up when they got gourmet, and sundaes for dessert. Over his coffee my father, who was a big reminiscer, told me all about Miriam Cobb, a band singer he'd been in love with years before he met my mother, for whom on many a cold winter evening he had cranked up his crank-up car to motor over from Princeton to the east side of Manhattan. "I loved her," my father said, a little tear welling in his eye, "but finally she told me she had to marry someone who was going to be a wheel."

37

Then he told me about Nancy, with whom he hadn't been in love at all. "I'll say this for Nancy, poor girl, she really loved me," my father recalled, "but I got to say, she was a little tacky." Whenever he talked about his old girlfriends, you got the point pretty fast about which girls he slept with and which ones he didn't.

But that was two years ago, and now I was nearly sixteen and very cool about dropping by the old mental hospital to watch a game or to get a free driving lesson around the grounds from Spencer or some other scruffy patient or hospital aide (half the time you couldn't tell the two groups apart). Brookhill was beautiful, even with the leaves gone, with rolling views and glistening ponds, and I loved going for a visit because there were all these cute, depressed guys hanging around. In my book, if a guy had long, dirty hair and looked like he had tuberculosis, he was halfway there. It was pretty hard to strike up any kind of relationship with anyone, though, what with the really good ones getting locked up at night.

Saturday afternoons Spencer and I would drive into Cambridge to sit around in the squalor of Harry's apartment and talk against the parents. It was my mother who was the primary target (my father generally escaping our criticism, except as a member of the parental unit)—my mother, who had devoted her life to being den and Brownie mother and to helping scores of kids create Christmas presents for their parents by sprinkling glitter over star-shaped ashtrays from the five-and-ten, who had lain awake at night trying to figure out how to be fair and spend the same exact amount on each child for Christmas, who had worried each hour of the day about what was the correct thing to do in order to bring us up as happy, mature adults. It was our mother we called "the phony" and "the social climber" because, I suppose, she had a lot of friends. When I'd come back from boarding school I'd been painfully nice to the parents, clearing the dishes every night in the special way they taught you at Greenfield, holding the knife and fork against the plate, but then I'd discovered the power I had of making Harry and Spencer laugh when I made fun of Mother. The parents had gone from being nice country club people to concerned liberals that year and my mother had become something of a philosopher.

"Life does funny things," she would muse at Sunday dinner and I would take her by the hand and look at her deeply.

"Mother," I would say, "you have opened my eyes." Even the brothers agreed that I was cruel, but they laughed, they couldn't help it, and I felt so guilty I only got worse.

"What *does* Mother do all day, anyway?" we would ask one another as we lounged around Harry's apartment, referring to the fact that Anita came in every Wednesday to clean, and finally we decided all she did was the laundry.

Before his breakdown Harry had been neat as a pin and helpful as could be around the house. When we were growing up my mother had worked out this complicated system, called, alluringly, The Chores, to teach us responsibility, which we had all groaned about, except for Harry, who would always do extra with the lightest of hearts. "Harry, would you please make our bed this morning?" Mother would ask. "Yes, master," Harry would say as a kind of joke, although where the humor was now escapes me, and when he was done you could bounce a quarter on it. But now it was all Harry could do to climb out of his dirt-stiff jeans before he went to sleep, and his apartment was so sloppy you couldn't see the floor. You had to wade through motorcycle parts and old Chinese food cartons and piles of dirty clothes to get over to the bed, and when you got there it was filled with peanut-butter cracker wrappers, and if you turned on the light above the pillow, it was rigged so that up on the record player would come *A Man and a Woman*.

Spencer and I would clear off a space on the frayed, brown plaid couch my parents had bought in the fifties, with the big buttons that killed your back, and smoke cigarettes while Harry paced around through the debris, cooking up hamburger or eating it raw out of the icebox, playing his saxophone when the spirit moved him and talking about how depressed he was. Harry had just dropped out of Harvard again, after a couple of months of halfheartedly attending classes. He had dropped out the first time when he'd cracked up two years earlier, and it had taken him that long before he'd been able to make himself go back. He had signed up for some philosophy courses that September, but he'd hated the assistant professor who'd made stupid comments and given him C's. "An Answer to Mr. Gilchrist," Harry had written as his last paper, taking each one of the assistant professor's remarks and tearing its logic to shreds. He'd received a B plus on the essay with no comments, and later, when Harry had happened to see him on Boylston Street, Gilchrist had risked his life to avoid him, fleeing to the other side of the street against a great wave of traffic. Then, a week before he turned twenty-one in December, Harry had quit school, even after the head of the Philosophy Department had said he hated to lose one of Harvard's brightest minds. *Where was he earlier?* Harry had wondered but, anyway, it didn't matter—something had happened to his dream of becoming an academic philosopher and winning prestigious fellowships, something had died inside of him, he didn't know why, and now he awoke every morning with a sinking, desperate feeling and he had to talk himself out of a panic all day just to make it to evening, when with an incredible effort he left the apartment to go out and buy a TV dinner.

If only he could fall in love, Harry explained to Spencer and me. Harry had just discovered that he could get a girl interested by bringing her to a bar where he was playing, and one night he had lured someone he'd had a big crush on for a year back to his apartment, suddenly eager to jump in the sack. But then, Harry said, he had started thinking about how the girl would have to leave in the morning to go to work, and how he would be all alone again, and he couldn't stop thinking about it, and he had gotten so depressed at the thought he had blown the whole thing and the girl had sensed it and had left within a half hour.

Generally, after a pack of Camels, Spencer would go out to Harvard Square and walk moodily by Club 47, while I remained behind, listening to Harry, as I watched the afternoon turn to night through the grimy windows of his gloomy apartment and wondered what in the world I could do to make him feel better. Harry said he was lonelier now than he had ever been—even lonelier than the summer before he flipped out, when the parents had sent him to Europe after a breakup with Corbin, his high school girlfriend. Harry had split up with Corbin in the middle of his freshman year, around the time he'd started being unhappy at Harvard, but right before he was leaving the country there'd been signs of a reconciliation. The parents had thought it best to stick to the original plan, however, and Harry had gone off to Europe, where he'd wandered miserably around by himself for two months, playing his clarinet in the streets and passing the hat, returning home with most of the money the parents had given him. Harry didn't see Corbin again for two years and then he ran into her one evening that fall when he was out buying a turkey TV dinner, and he wondered to himself what all the fuss had been about. Corbin, on the other hand, had cried when she'd visited Harry's apartment. "What are you crying about?" Harry had asked, but Corbin said she didn't know, it was just sad.

I fizzed cigarette ashes over half-empty Tab cans those cold weekends as Harry went on and on about how he had tried to become a radical or at least a liberal and support Eugene McCarthy, but couldn't seem to get motivated, and how the only time all year he hadn't been tired and depressed was when he'd seen the movie *The Pawnbroker,* and then he'd felt a little happy that somebody else had felt worse.

Harry was always, always depressed, and all I wanted in life was for him to get undepressed, but Harry didn't believe in shrinks. Look at the shrink at Harvard who had prescribed him speed before his breakdown, he said. The doctors thought

41

speed was a wonder drug then, and every day for two months it had been strongly advised for Harry, his heart pumping furiously, to swallow the lethal amphetamine, until finally, completely worn down, he had contracted pneumonia. It was only right after the pneumonia he had gone stark-raving mad, Harry pointed out, maintaining the mental collapse would never have taken place without the physical one, and blaming all the suffering that was to follow on the quackery of the psychiatric profession.

I was barely sixteen, and I hadn't a clue about what had really happened, let alone whom to blame for what, though deep inside I think I yearned for the comfort of a faith in psychiatry and its ability to heal, a faith that was as necessary to my mother's besieged family as air to breathe. But I wasn't about to argue with Harry, who had been through so much I still dared not ask about, so instead I listened and listened to him, as he talked about how down he was, and then, finally, on the upswing, about this waitress at Elsie's delicatessen who had brought him a cup of soup.

"I think she really understands," Harry said, "and she's got really great legs."

I didn't have a single friend in high school that fall—I felt as if my profound suffering had removed me to a loftier plane from that of my classmates—and I was proud of being alone. Only the year before I had dreamed of becoming a cheerleader, to the horror of the parents, but now I viewed the vivacious, popular girls with pity as they rushed to the shallowness of basketball games and senior bake sales, while I roamed the hallways in my Indian-print skirts and dark-circled eyes. I had managed to work up a bit of insomnia; many nights I would lie in bed until two, staring at the pink budding flowers on my bedroom wall, wallpaper I had begged for but that now seemed a little silly. One night I got the brilliant idea of noisily swallowing five aspirin in the parents' bathroom, plunking the aspirin bottle down hard on the glass shelves, but even my mother, who would wake up with a start at the mere thought of a roast beef that would need to be taken from the freezer the next day, miraculously slept on.

In class, I wrote inarticulate essays about faceless faces who let down their armor only to put it back on again, upon which my kind but weak sophomore English teacher would comment, "Interesting . . . I don't quite follow you here." When we did the expository essay, and how the opening paragraph was like a triangle upside down, and passed our work around the class, my paper explained, ". . . her body lying hot in the sun, suddenly eclipsed by his . . . and then down he came and their bodies became as one," as if my body went around becoming one with guys at the drop of a pin. Even the sophomore boys, who giggled at the vaguest innuendo and called out "pork" whenever Miss Joyceln turned to write on the board, were silenced by that one.

Spencer and Harry had told me it was dishonest not to sleep with a guy if you loved him, and I took it gravely to heart. *If only he knew,* I'd think ironically as I passed Robert Whipler and the eternally tanned Deb Soblosksy downtown, laughing as they went off to the hypocritical third base. I solemnly informed the parents that I intended to live with a man before I married him. We were all very grown up about it, which wasn't too hard, seeing I didn't even go out on a date till Christmas, if you can call sitting in Towney Forrester's room making out to "And then along comes Mary . . ." going out on a date. Towney Forrester's mother let him bring girls into his bedroom, though he had to leave the door open, not that this had the slightest cautioning effect on Towney. Kiss, kiss, kiss, we'd go, lying side by side on his bed as his mother or his father or his older sister bustled by, not more than three feet away. Towney was a hip preppy with long, lanky hair and the face of a dog, and at age sixteen he must have lain in a prone position, in the bosom of his family, with half the pretty girls in Concord. He wasn't good-looking and he wasn't smart, he went to Chauncy, which is where you went if you

43

couldn't get into Andover, but he had "it," as my father would have said. Also, nobody was hip in public school yet, and he was the first guy I'd met besides my brothers who was. I don't even know how I found him, as I never hung out with the private school set, but I think the only reason he was interested in me was because he admired Spencer, who played guitar— Towney himself had a set of drums in his room, which he banged away at from time to time when we came up for air. After a passionate Christmas vacation together, Towney went back to school, having left me with an invitation for the Chauncy winter dance.

I don't know whether it was the weekly box of cookies I shipped off, leaving out a plate of burned rejects for my father every Friday afternoon, or the long, precious letters with the circle-dotted *i*'s and the triple asterisks I flooded him with ("If found by person return by mail, if found by male return in person!" I amusingly wrote on one envelope), but the week before the dance, Towney called me to tell me he had a paper due, so I'd better not come up.

"Oh, that's all right," I said, "I'll just bring a book."

"I'll have to study all weekend, it won't be any fun," Towney warned.

"Oh, I don't mind, I just want to see *you!*" I assured him, and so up I went, Spencer driving me in the old Saab to the town of Andover.

"Have fun," said Spencer with a little pat on my back as he left me off at the temporary girls' dorm.

Friday night was dinner at the headmaster's, where Towney made in-jokes with his friends and seemed irritated with my existence. He was mad at me about my hair, for one thing, which admittedly was in an awkward stage. You were supposed to have long, straight hair if you were cool, but I had been cool only since September and my hair was still growing out of a bubble cut, and I'd pulled it back with one of those phosphorescent headbands you got six to a card at the five-

and-ten. After dinner I sat awkwardly by the fire in the living room, not knowing how to arrange my body, and felt a lump rising in my throat.

"Why are you holding on to yourself?" Towney asked, referring to my hands, which I thought were so decorously folded in my lap. "I hate it when girls do that, as if they can't find anyone else to hold hands with."

"Oh," I said and moved them apart an inch as if they were blocks of wood. Towney didn't kiss me good night and then the next day he suggested I go to the hockey game without him, as he had to study.

"No problem," I said cheerily, "I'll come up and read," and so he reluctantly smuggled me up to his cell on the third floor.

I sank back blissfully in the corner of Towney's bed, my back against the wall, reading in the late afternoon sun, while Towney sat at his desk making motions of studying, a little mixed-up about whether he was supposed to have a paper due or an exam. First he opened one book, then another, then he got out a pad of paper, then he scraped his chair back and got up and stood by the window. Finally he came over to me on the bed. I went farther with Towney in that stuffy little room than ever I had gone before. Gladly would I have gone the whole way with him. Gladly would I have given my life for him, flung my body across train tracks before a speeding train if need be, I thought, as I lay beside him, my fingers caressing his temple, and then he said, "If you don't stop rubbing me in that place, you'll burn a hole in my skin," and got up and stomped back to his desk.

At the dance that night Towney seemed transfixed by his best friend's date, who was pretty only because her hair worked, and the next morning I announced I thought I might leave right after breakfast. I prayed that Towney would say, "No, no, stay here, with me!" as you pray when they pass back the math exam you haven't studied for that you'll miraculously receive an A, but of course it was not to be so. I called up Spencer and when he arrived he found me in the woods off the quad huddled in a little heap, face-down on the snow crust.

"Well, I guess you didn't have such a good time," Spencer said and, putting his arm around me, walked me back to the car.

I was bitter about Towney Forrester for quite some time, or, anyway, for a month and a half, and drew strength from my bitterness. *I'll show him,* I thought, and came up with a daring plan. After weeks of planning, I finally ran across him at a party during the private schools' spring vacation. He was sitting on a couch entwined with Mare Hawkes, a *saftig* blonde who became increasingly popular every year as the months got warmer because her family owned a pool. I parked myself across the room and threw them withering looks, which I thought were pretty dramatic until someone asked me if I was going to be sick. You need cheekbones to throw withering looks, and my face and features were rounded, attractive as a whole in a red-cheeked, salacious sort of way (I'd started out life with my mother's sharp New England outlines but somewhere along the line they'd been blunted by my father's cuteness), but in need of a cheery aspect. Finally I got up my courage and marched over to Towney on the couch.

"I have something to say to you," I croaked in a low voice.

"Sure, honey, have a seat," he said, patting the couch. I sat down into the pillowy cushion, then leaned over and cupped my hand to his ear.

"Fuck you!" I whispered fiercely.

"Good for you!" replied Towney with what amounted to a slap on the back, and, mortified, I skulked away, never, as it turned out, to set eyes on Towney Forrester again.

It was with a superior air that I stalked the halls of the high school that spring, wearing miniskirts now and a thick blob of black on my upper eyelids. No one spoke to me but the hoods who cheered as I passed by and called out from their revved-up cars, "Hey, Lizzie!" for, I thought, no apparent reason, overlooking the fact that every time I washed my orange sweater dress it got shorter and tighter. Everyone in my high school was still wearing the muted colors and gathered waists of the fifties, and the bright colors and short skirts that were beginning to be worn in Harvard Square were, at least to me, full of great social significance.

Then, in May, I went to the Armory Sociable.

The Armory Sociable was a dance sponsored by a group of mothers; it wasn't quite as snobby as the country club affairs, but it was a private dance and one you went to without a date. I had sat out in the yard all day and had a beautiful red-gold tan and a lightheaded feeling. Most of the kids at the Sociable went to private school and I knew them only by sight from the country club, but that night it didn't bother me. I took a place at one of the white-clothed tables, my legs stretched before me in my long, cotton Merimekko dress (a little hipper than chiffon) with spaghetti straps, feeling, frankly, rather beautiful. *How can anyone even look at me? They will be blinded by my beauty* is the line along which I was thinking, which was one way to deal with the fact that no one was asking me to dance. I moved my face gracefully from side to side, watching the dancers pant away, doing the pony or the frug awkwardly in their formal clothes, the girls' legs beating valiantly, but to no avail, against the constraints of their long gowns. There was Warren Billings, tanned already and more handsome than ever, still squiring Sally Ames around, who, I was happy to note, danced like a windshield wiper. But I was above hatred now and benignly I smiled upon them, one and all. Then, halfway through the dance, I saw Spencer standing in the Armory doorway and, next to him, Pony Raker.

They looked like wrecks, of course, in their frayed corduroys and rumpled work shirts, their pupils dilated with marijuana, but to me they were heroes to the rescue in a sea of white jackets and madras cummerbunds. I floated out to them and without a word Pony and I moved off in a dream, dancing

47

slowly on the outskirts of the floor, leaving Spencer to fend off the hearty braggings of Mr. Hardigan, who for some reason was present that night as a chaperone, even though his son Fritz, who had stolen the one girl Spencer had ever really cared about, had already graduated with Spencer's class and gone on to Yale, where, Spencer was delighted to be informed that night, he had made Dean's List as well as varsity crew.

Finally Pony and I completed our revolution and, after we picked up Spencer, the three of us glided out into the parking lot. "Wow," said Pony, as Spencer turned on the headlights in the old Saab, "this is like being inside a spaceship," and then we drove back home to the playroom, where, in the red light, we lay on the couches watching TV, making vague, deep comments from time to time.

"Those boots are filled with Pony," I said dizzily and, I thought, rather poetically, after staring at Pony's cowboy boots, which stood in the corner.

"It's like Lizzie's stoned, too," Pony murmured, conferring upon me the highest honor, and finally Spencer left us alone and we drifted into each other's arms.

Chapter Four

Harry had moved that spring to an apartment in Central Square, a less depressing part of Cambridge than Porter Square, which by summer he was sharing with William, who had just graduated from Harvard and was working in Cambridge before leaving for a term at the London School of Economics. William had roomed with Harry freshman and sophomore years, and it had been William who'd dragged him to the hospital when Harry'd flipped out. William was black, I suppose I should mention, although never in all the years I knew him did this ever seem to have the slightest effect on any of his actions.

William, who was always at the forefront of the latest trends, was already a Marxist, though in a refined, convivial, wine-drinking sort of way—even in his strictest radical phases he had his shirts dry-cleaned at the Gold Coast Valeteria. And yet it was William who, spying one day the volume of the family history, placed mercifully beyond reach on the parents' bookshelves, bestirred himself this once in his life down to the basement and up again with a ladder, in order to bring to our attention the fact that Priscilla Chittenden was, at the illustrious moment of touching her foot to Plymouth Rock, only twelve years old and not Priscilla *Chittenden* at all, but Priscilla *Caldwell,* with eight years to pass before she would give herself to Francis Chittenden, who, William felt obliged to report, did *not* come over on the Mayflower but on the *Fortune,* in the year following. William had a way, with his somewhat English accent, of discussing things, even the most boring subjects ("Indeed, it is the boring subjects that are so *challenging*"), that riveted one's attention.

For all the thousands of hours I was to spend sitting around the kitchen in Concord with William, talking on and on about nothing, I never once thought of asking him exactly what had happened when Harry had flipped out. Somehow it wasn't the kind of matter you wanted to pursue with William; you were too busy being gripped by the age-old debate of whether to cover a certain armchair of his in green or red, a question that might merit two and a half hours one Saturday afternoon and one hour the next, and that might have been better phrased (I realized on a later visit to William and Harry's slovenly abode): When was the soonest we could dash into town and deliver the chair to the nearest burning incinerator?

It occurred to me to ask about Harry's breakdown only many years later, and then William said the funny thing had been that it had taken so long for him to realize Harry was crazy. After all, everyone at Harvard was taking drugs, even in 1964, particularly around exam time, when any night of the week you might walk into their suite of rooms, turn on the light, and find Harry and William's other roommate, Morrie, a perfectly normal fellow except that he dressed only in black, sitting on top of the refrigerator. Anyway, William said that Harry had been a compulsive studier his freshman year, but in the fall of his sophomore year he suddenly stopped doing any work, William's and his friends' customary state, but Harry, having never been in this position, had panicked and, as the semester was drawing to a close, he'd gone to a shrink at the infirmary who prescribed him Dexamyl for the headache he'd had all fall and Dexedrine for the lethargy. No one, including the doctors, understood speed in those days; Morrie and William figured it was a glorified version of No-doz, and neither of them thought much about it as Harry continued to gobble the tablets down every day in order to write his paper on what one sentence that someone says to Krishna in the Bhagavad Gita meant; Harry always chose narrow subjects—it was his edge, and he would agonize over minutiae for pages on end. The paper got later and later and Harry continued to take the tablets and soon it began to become a matter of debate whether or not Harry had been to bed in recent memory. Harry looked awful, William said, but then everyone else did during exam period, and, when the term was over, his paper now hopelessly overdue, Harry took William up on his invitation to go to Albany to spend the intersession with William and his family.

Twenty minutes before the bus to Albany was due to leave, Harry went into the bathroom and found William, who had yet to pack, still in the shower. William, who never saw any need to hurry about anything, always showered for at least thirty minutes, even though generally the water would be freezing cold for the last fifteen.

"You don't expect me to travel without a shower?" William had protested, and by the time he and Harry, bags in hand, had reached the bus stop, the bus was disappearing around the corner. They'd proceeded to chase the bus for several blocks, making themselves hot with the effort, so when Harry suggested hitching, even though the temperature was near zero, William said the idea had not seemed amiss. Almost immediately they had gotten a lift from some guy on his way to Chicago, who dropped them off within thirty miles of Albany.

"Fantastic," William had said, but Harry, who was a veteran, having hitched around Europe the summer before, had replied tersely, "You're not there till you're there."

For four hours Harry and William had stood in the bitter cold, about twenty yards from the warmth and civilization of a tollbooth, and had watched hundreds of cars whiz by. Harry had turned literally blue, a thing William had never seen, and next William had realized he himself was no longer capable of putting his thumb out. It was so cold his arm was numb, and it fell down every time he tried to prop it up, and suddenly William had thought to himself, *We just might die here.* So they'd hobbled over to the tollbooth and begged their way in, and finally a car had stopped and given them a lift to William's house. It had taken them an entire day to feel warm again, and though William, who was basically healthy, recovered completely, Harry, who had seemed all right at William's house, contracted pneumonia when they got back to school, his resistance so low from the speed and the sleepless nights.

Harry had been taking a course that fall on the abnormal personality, but he hadn't read a word of the assigned reading until he was convalescing from the pneumonia in the infirmary, and then he couldn't put any of it down. He understood everything now, why he'd been so depressed that fall, he told William and Mother when they were visiting him. All these years he'd blamed himself for Mother's getting sick and leaving him when he was five, but, Harry now understood, it wasn't his fault and it wasn't Mother's fault. It was nobody's fault, and, now that he understood this, his mental problems were all over. And indeed, William said, Harry, who had been so sullen for months, now looked as if a tremendous load had been lifted off his shoulders. "Look at the trees outside, everything is so beautiful! I'm so happy now," Harry burst forth in a warm rush of emotion, embracing Mother, to whom he had hardly spoken a civil word in nearly a year, as she tried to smile, though obviously stricken from hearing for the first time that Harry had blamed himself all these years for her collapse.

Harry developed a kind of glow, and within a week he was out of the infirmary, seeming to have survived it all in tip-top shape. Everything was just dandy, until the Monday that he began his second-term philosophy tutorial on "The Good."

"What *is* the ultimate Good?" Harry asked, pacing around
the suite, and then late one night (one still never knew, William said, when or if Harry went to bed), he strode into the
bedroom William shared with Morrie and started talking to
the sleeping Morrie as if they were already in the middle of an
animated conversation.

"You're the smartest person I know and you've got to figure
it out—it's about this course I'm going to teach at Harvard
when I become a full professor, and I can't do it until I know
what *is* 'The Good,' " Harry said, rousing Morrie, and then
he proceeded to go on and on, in a confused and excited state,
while William, who at eighteen was young for his class, and
had never seen anything like this, pretended he had not been
awakened and cowered in his bed.

"I can't sleep," Harry said frantically. "I'm afraid to go to
sleep because I'm afraid my heart is going to stop," and on
and on he continued the entire night, storming out at dawn.
William didn't know what to make of any of it, and the next
day, which was a Saturday, when William returned from an
errand, there was Harry sprawled out full length on the sofa,
while on its edge sat two chirpy, perfumed-up Wellesley girls
to whom he was explaining, in rather a compelling fashion to
judge by the spellbound look on the girls' faces, that in fact
he was the Holy Ghost and, for that matter, always had been.
And yet, William said, though he thought it all rather odd,
he had by now become almost accustomed to Harry's ravings
and wasn't greatly alarmed until later that afternoon, when he
related these experiences to a couple of friends, who kept
interrupting him as the story went on.

"Harry? Harry Reade?" they kept asking. "This is really
flipped out." Then the discussion had turned to what ought
to be done, with the conclusion that the whole thing had gone
beyond supportive actions by roommates being of any use and
that Harry should go back to the infirmary. When the group
of them had returned to the suite, Harry was still explaining
to the girls on the couch why he was at least the spirit of God,

if not the man himself. There had been a slight fear that Harry would resist, with him being so big, but when William suggested in an offhand manner that Harry might want to check in at the infirmary, he had offered no argument whatsoever.

To the doctors at the infirmary, however, Harry didn't look as harmless as he had to his friends, and the first thing the orderlies did was strap the ranting Harry onto a stretcher and wheel him away, with William trying to follow and explain that Harry wasn't dangerous. William later learned from a girl who was in the infirmary at the time with mono that Harry's shouting about The Good and Lynne Anne May (a notoriously libertine girl in Harry's tutorial, who, it was alleged, once stopped a Harvard guy in the midst of sex, saying, "A hundred bucks") had been heard all over the building for the rest of the day. The next morning, when William came to visit, a cop was stationed in Harry's room, although Harry seemed to be allowed to venture forth, at least as far as the lounge, where he could stand with arms straight out, screaming, "Don't crucify me!" and make a number of rousing speeches ("I came to Harvard to search for *Veritas,* but what did I find?"), but, unfortunately, nobody was present.

William said when he rang my mother to break it to her that Harry seemed to be ill and in a bit of a mental collapse, she had seemed completely calm, as if this was all par for the course, saying, "Thank you so very much for all your help," and that she and Mr. Reade would come right in and sort things out. (Not so calm, my father revealed, when he testified later about the phone call she had made to him immediately following William's. My father had been at Grant's department store, in the middle of making a deal for a huge shipment of mattresses with his most difficult client, when Mother had reached him. "We've got to take Harry to the lunatic asylum!" my father alleges she said, though my mother still takes issue with the wording. My father said he burst into tears right there on the phone, but when it really hit was when he arrived at Stillman Infirmary and found Harry, who had been so rebellious all fall, now meek as a lamb, sobbing and pleading with him: "I just want you to take me home and take care of me.")

In the ambulance over to Brookhill, William said he hadn't been able to look at my mother's face as she struggled to be strong and do the right thing, as her son, still baby-faced at nineteen, cried out to her, bestowing on her the last compliments he would give her in many years: "I love you, Mother, I really do. I just want to go home. Just take me home. Don't take me to this place. Please, Mom, you're such a good cook; I love your cooking, Mom, you can take care of me, please let me come home with you and Dad."

But there had been nothing else that could be done and Harry had been committed at Brookhill, not to be released until the following fall. And now, two and a half years later, he was rooming with William again.

Chapter Five

William and Harry allowed me to come in anytime I wanted and cook them French toast and tidy up the apartment. I'd been cleaning Harry's rooms kind of on and off for a year, taking the train from Concord to grungy Porter Square near Sears and soaring down Mass. Ave., past the sleazy bars and pizza places, with the lightest step, thinking the whole way that if somehow I could just get it so that Harry could see the floor he would feel better. The original theory was that I was to be paid for cleaning up, but after the first time I'd done it, Harry had said it made him feel funny to give his sister money and that had been that.

Throughout the summer the parents went away every weekend to a cabin they had on a lake in New Hampshire, which they had bought the year before with the fifteen thousand dollars left from my grandmother's money after paying Brookhill to find out their children's problems were all their fault. ("I didn't ask to be born!" had been the line Spencer and Harry had found effective as a show-stopper in fights with the parents.) Harry had said he couldn't understand why, instead of buying the cabin, they hadn't just divided up the money among us kids. Harry, Spencer, and I hated the little bungalow, with the framed, pressed flowers on the wall, and the only one of us kids who went up there on a regular basis was George.

"How can you stand it up there?" we asked him. "It's so bourgeois!" But George took the seven-hour bus trip up from New York several times that summer for the incomprehensible reason that he liked seeing the parents—even if it meant you couldn't sit quietly inside and read a book without a lot of bitterness in the air that you weren't out enjoying the lake and sailing on the new secondhand Sailfish upon which, at age fifty, my father had just learned to sail. George said he'd be just settling into the couch with the newspaper after helping with the breakfast dishes when he'd hear the clank-clank of the boom and the flap-flap of the canvas and then my father's voice calling out, "Anyone for a sail?"

"No, thank you!" George would answer cheerily, as if to say, gee, he really wanted to but he couldn't make it this one time.

"It would please your father so much if you would go for a ride with him," my mother would urge in a low voice.

"What's the matter with you that you don't want to sail?" my father would ask George irritably, and off he would teeter by himself onto the waters of Lake Wabasso, whistling through his teeth and looking like a senator on vacation, with his yellow-silver hair and erect posture. My mother and I had refused to sail with him after he had tipped us over once and ruined our hairs, so the only companion he ever had was Scout, who stood up the whole time and generally capsized the boat.

"Stay, stay," my father would command the dog on the beach as he pushed off from shore, but Scout, ever loyal if by then blind, would jump in and flail about drowningly. "Go home, go home!" my father would call out over and over from the boat, his voice bouncing off the water into screened windows all around the lake, until finally he would lift the pant-

58

ing dog on board, and the blue-and-white sail would wobble once with a clang and disappear from sight.

Scout always went to New Hampshire with the parents, but Aphrodite, goddess of love, was not invited. Aphro, though fixed, had remained highly sexed, and on the weekends, without poor, unreceptive Scout to hurl herself against, she had set her sights on Spencer, weaving her lovers' web with a few salacious wriggles and piercing yaps and closing in one Friday night when, after jumping on Spencer while he was watching TV, lying on the couch, she squatted and peed on his back. I observed the courtship from another corner of the room, waiting patiently for the warm fluid to penetrate the layers of Spencer's clothes. "That's it!" he cried when finally it dawned upon him what had happened, and although Aphrodite continued, with the mounting passion of unrequited love, to desire Spencer in the years to come, losing all control of her bladder at the mere sound of his voice in the next room, Spencer, who loved dogs more than his life, never recognized the existence of Aphro again.

We thought our scorn for their New Hampshire cabin must have withered the parents, but how nice it must have been, I realize now, for them to get a break from us. The sixties were a dim decade for my parents. While all their friends were coming back from Europe to show you 150 slides of different members of their family waving merrily from the same Italian rock, the parents were busy picking us up at schools we no longer attended and having little chats with psychiatrists about where exactly they'd gone wrong. For two months my mother had driven over to Brookhill to discuss, at fifty bucks a whack, how her supposed "rape" by the plumber (poor old Mr. Katzmiller from the Cherry Lane apartments, the sweetest man who ever lived, according to Mother) had affected Harry, even after all agreed nothing even vaguely resembling the incident had ever occurred.

My mother said the idea of blaming herself hadn't dawned on her until the chief psychiatrist had sat her down a couple

59

of weeks after Harry's breakdown and said, "The first thing I want to say is very important: I don't want you and Mr. Reade to feel guilty, and I'm assigning you to a social worker." The social worker was twenty-two and had a giant gap between her front teeth.

"Now, Mr. and Mrs. Reade," she would lisp concernedly at eight-thirty every Wednesday and Friday morning, as my father tried not to worry about being late at the office, "how do you *feel* about Harry being sick?" and on and on. One day my mother happened to ask when the last time she'd seen Harry was. "Oh!" the social worker cried, "I make it a point to *never* meet the patient!"

Never discussed was why the rest of us children, with the same parents and similar experiences, hadn't also gone stark raving mad; the possibility of genetic predisposition was not considered. It was what the parents had done, and they had no choice but to listen, because without the experts there was no hope. They'd geared their life to bringing us up, and as well they might have patted each other on the back for our early successes, now they shouldered the guilt of what must have been the errors of their ways with a grim grace.

As it turned out, of course, my parents' problems with their children were the forerunners of bad things that seemed eventually to befall so many of the families in Concord. Now you go home for a visit and hear in a hushed whisper how the Bibbins' daughter, who was so snappy and so soft-hearted she cried to see a puppy with a thorn in its paw, had ditched her husband and infant twins, and run away with the guy who'd fixed the washing machine. But, in 1967, when it came to being in people's whispers, we were tops.

With the parents gone on summer weekends, everyone came out to Concord: Pony, Harry, William, and Spencer, who had only recently moved out of the house and was driving a cab and sharing Pony's apartment in Brighton with the fake pine paneling. In a great turnaround, the parents had suddenly decided Spencer was all well, after his psychiatrist had said, "Hey, let's face it, Spencer can't sing," which, even if it had been true, was not the way to warm up to my father, who, through thick and thin, was always a big bragger about us kids. With two kids in and out of the loony bin, and another dropping out of school, my father could still turn to someone at a party and say, "My son George just got a raise at his part-time job."

All weekend long, the five of us would sit in the yellow kitchen at the yellow Formica table, one meal blending into the next as we talked and talked, toking up every few hours. I had been allowed to join the ranks and had a puff or two now and then and got high, or I think I got high. I had also gotten high smoking banana skins, which Spencer and I broiled one Monday afternoon in the oven, right in front of Mother, who couldn't say anything in that it was legal. We stayed in the kitchen all weekend mainly because William liked to linger leisurely over his food, which we thought was so gourmet until one day we realized that he really just talked away until the food was ice cold, then wolfed it down, one, two, three. The main activity was watching me bake the brownies and cakes I made because Mother didn't, although one time we all got up the energy to go over to the country club to play tennis. It took us about three hours to get organized, and, when we arrived at the club, I in neat white shorts, the others in cut-off versions of their usual rags, unshaven and hair looking like they'd just stuck their fingers in a socket, we got a startled look from the members, and then a smile as they decided, I suppose, that I was engaged in some kind of social work. In the evenings we'd drag ourselves up from the kitchen table to go sit up on the second floor of the barn and play *Sergeant Pepper's Lonely Hearts Club Band,* our legs dangling out of the hayloft as we watched Maple Street go by.

"Wow," we'd say when a woman walked by with her dog, and then marvel at the acuteness of our perception.

61

We were all rather cool and laid back, except for Harry, who, when he got high, only got more intense.

"Mother doesn't talk *to* you, she talks *at* you," he said one day as we were eating hot, soupy cheesecake. ("Wow, this is great," said Pony, "really different," when of course it was just that we had forgotten that you were supposed to refrigerate it.)

Yeah, yeah, Harry, we agreed, dipping our spoons.

"I don't think you understand the full ramifications of my statement," Harry returned warmly, and it took us a half hour to convince him we did.

Then there was the book Harry was going to write about starting a diet fast-food restaurant. "It would sell, you know it would sell," he kept insisting, and finally after writing a page or two, he turned to me and said, "You know, maybe I should be writing a book about something I *know*," as if it were a brilliant conclusion.

Pony and I had, since the Armory Sociable, gotten pretty romantic. I was on the record about honesty meaning sleeping with someone you loved, and one afternoon my mother came into my room and kind of fidgeted around concernedly.

"Mom," I said, though of recent years I had been calling her Mother in a pointed manner, in order to keep the lines drawn, "I'm not sleeping with Pony."

"Oh, thank you, thank you," my mother said joyfully, "I didn't want to ask, it's just you're so young," and she walked out of the room with a little dance. My mother was big on trusting you to do the right thing, but you couldn't blame her for worrying, what with my definition of integrity and vanishing skirts.

"Lizzie may *seem* very grown up," she had taken William aside one day to say—everybody in my family always forgetting I was "Elizabeth" now—"but remember she is only sixteen." William got along great with Mother—he always said he never understood why she was the one we jumped all over.

I wasn't quite sure if I was in love with Pony, and because he was gracious he had not pushed, though we did continue to do a bit of grappling around on the playroom couch. One night my father came home late from playing his banjo at a party and walked right into the playroom without a knock. My mother had a rule that you could go with boyfriends or girlfriends into the playroom and shut the door, on the theory that it was less likely to lead to trouble than parking, but how effective this rule was I cannot say, as that night Pony and I were lying on the couch wearing nothing but an old army blanket that was Scout's.

"Hello, Mr. Reade," said Pony brightly, and I mean brightly, in that Pony had elected to turn on the lamp next to us and crane its goose neck so that one hundred watts streamed into our faces and down our blanketed, intertwined bodies.

"Hello, Pony. Hello, Lizzie," my father greeted us as casually as if he'd met us riding our bikes down the street, and then he banged around for a while putting his banjo away and went up to bed. All that night I tossed and turned in my pink sheets in my pink room wondering what my father was thinking about his daughter, whom heretofore, against considerable evidence, he had thought perfect.

"Lizzie may be beautiful, but it's too bad she's not bright!" and "Lizzie's so bright, it's too bad she's not good-looking!" he used to say with a big wink—before the night he opened the playroom door without a knock. Always, I had been beautiful in his eyes: as a little girl in a barbershop pixie with a pinched, anemic face, as an adolescent in sloppy clothes to hide my suddenly buxom body. In the mirror I looked like someone had left the top drawer open in a chest of drawers, but my father, my father lay awake in bed terrified that the owners of *Playboy* magazine would come in the night and tear me from my home. "Lizzie, promise your dear old father you will never be Miss June," he had begged me, and more than once.

So I did not know what to expect the next morning as I walked by the parents' room, but what I found was my father whistling away and shining his shoes as he always did, the dozen tins of brown polish lined up neatly along a spread-out newspaper. I was not particularly chipper in the morning as a rule, but my father made a habit of cheerily calling out good morning when I passed him on my way to the bathroom, and I would grumble something, and he would say, " 'Good morning, father dear, how lovely to see you!' " and go back to whistling through his teeth. That morning, though, I stopped at his door and stood there trying to act natural.

"Great Dixieland music at the Chase's last night, if I do say so myself," my father said, giving his shoes a buff, "and you should have seen your mother doing the fast dances. She really wowed them." No one did the twist any longer but my mother, who churned her tall, statuesque body up and down with a ferocious expression on her face. We chatted a little and finally my father said, "You young like to listen to records lying down, I guess; can't say that I blame you," and that was the end of it.

In the fall Pony went back to M.I.T. and I went back to Concord High. It was easy being a hippie in the summer, but sitting in class thinking vague thoughts and not paying attention was a little boring, with the result that I quit smoking pot and stopped eating anything worth more than sixty calories and turned the zeal of my self-denial mercilessly upon my schoolwork. ("That Lizzie Reade is so austere," I heard one girl whisper to another in the dressing rooms after gym, but the truth was, I was just starving myself to death.) So it was rather a surprise that winter when the doorbell rang at our house, and there, as Mother opened the door, stood Sergeant McNulty, chief of the Concord police, looking for me.

"This is a little awkward, Mrs. Reade," Sergeant McNulty addressed my mother, who stood there looking kempt and beautiful in her mother hairdo and tan slacks, "but a charge

64

has been made against your daughter, Elizabeth, and I wondered if I might talk to her."

"Why, of course, Sergeant McNulty, come right in. Lizzie, Ben, Sergeant McNulty is here!" she called merrily up the stairs, as if some long-lost cousin had dropped by for a surprise visit. We all gathered in the living room and a nicer little family you never did see.

"It seems," said Sergeant McNulty, while my mother and father looked on expectantly, "that a charge has been made— I received the call yesterday—that Elizabeth here has been uh dealing among uh the Concord youths uh drugs." It turned out that Mr. Duncan, who taught shop at the high school and with whom I had never so much as exchanged a single word, had inexplicably reported me to the police. Luckily I had already informed my parents that I had smoked pot, so I was now able to stand up and make a stirring speech about how I had tried marijuana, as any member of our generation was apt to do—though certainly I had never sold it to others—but I had found it interfered in the life of a responsible individual and given it up. There was a little round of applause from the parents and coffee was had by all and finally Sergeant McNulty slunk away.

I broke up with Pony that spring. It was an unpleasant evening, with Pony reminiscing about our romance and me sitting there cold as can be, not a feeling on me. Over and over I have remembered that moment when I have been on the other end, crying as if my heart would break, while my rejector was probably looking over my shaking shoulder at his watch and wondering if he could gracefully make his exit before the pizza place closed. At last, after a long kiss goodbye, Pony returned to Cambridge.

"Well," I thought to myself as I nestled cozily into *The Protestant Ethic and the Spirit of Capitalism* that night, "that's over." But then a week later I received a phone call from Pony.

"I'm coming out to see you this afternoon," he said grimly, and there was no arguing him out of it.

65

I watched Pony with his red lumber jacket and long face trudge through the rain down the sidewalk and up to the front porch. In silence I let him in the door and escorted him to the living room.

"Spencer says you love me," said Pony.

"Well," I replied matter-of-factly, "Spencer is wrong."

Chapter Six

In the middle of my junior year I had suddenly decided that I wanted to go to Radcliffe, rather to the alarm of my guidance counselor, whom I had assured loftily the previous September, a daisy set meaningfully behind my ear, that I had no intention of going to college at all. For the next several Machiavellian months I was far too busy joining yearbook committee meetings and singing "Ooooh-oklahoma!" bonneted, in the chorus of the school play, and teaching slow kids math in a program called Reaching Backwards to see much of Harry or Spencer, who, currently uninstitutionalized, were putting all their energies into making it in the music world. Their musical career together had continued pretty much uninterrupted from the aftermath of Harry's breakdown, when they had tentatively launched themselves as a group at the Catacombs, through Spencer's more nebulous mental collapse. Spencer had sung and played guitar with Harry on sax or flute at the social functions Brookhill always seemed to be having (to cheer everyone up, I guess, with bitter songs about reality), and after Spencer had left the hospital, the June of my sophomore year, they'd played for peanuts in coffeehouses around Harvard

Square. But Spencer and Harry's first real break didn't come until the following summer, the summer before my senior year, when Spencer was twenty and Harry twenty-two, and a scout from a big record label invited them down to New York to make a demo tape with the view of cutting their own album.

Spencer was so nervous during the session, he told me afterward, he'd had to keep excusing himself to go drink hot water cupped in his hands in the men's room, especially after some technician helpfully mentioned they were recording in the same studio Bob Dylan worked in. But it had gone well, Harry and Spencer felt, and when they came home they kept talking about what it would be like being famous together.

It was Spencer who got the phone call two days later.

"We want you," said the guy from the record company, "but your brother can't come along,"

"No way," Spencer said, and hung up the phone.

"You're nuts," Harry kept telling him later.

"I'm not being noble or anything," Spencer replied, "I just know I can't do it without you, I'm no good without you, without you I'd just shrivel up." And it was true Spencer had never played anywhere without Harry, whom he'd looked up to as a musician for so many years, since Spencer was ten, beating his sticks on that piece of wood they gave you to see if you wanted to play drums, since he was eight, playing "Long, long a-go, long, long a-go" on the Flutophone, since Spencer had even been sure he could play anything at all.

"Well, you're nuts; I'd go if I were you," said Harry, who always meant what he said, and, a man of his word, it was Harry who left Spencer and went off to New York that fall, to record with Tim Hardin.

Harry was still in New York in December when we received a letter from him addressed to all of us that said "Do not open 'til December 25th!" This seemed a miracle, coming from Harry, who never gave presents unless I went out and bought them for him, and then, of course, he forgot to get one for me. In fact, Christmas had been going along so smoothly that year, you could almost have been smug about it. Usually Mother and I would get all excited about the brothers coming home, the glow of Christmas in our hearts as we made from scratch the eggnog nobody liked as well as the kind in the carton and put out the crèche with the fake hay and the little china figurines—and then everyone would arrive and get in a big fight about stringing the lights on the tree. But that year Spencer, who was "so mechanical!" having once tightened the wires on a stereo speaker while the rest of us prayed for his dear life, strung the lights by himself while George played Christmas carols on the piano with hardly any mistakes. "Why can't he go out and play baseball?" my father had said in response to George's piano practicing as a young boy, but George was the only one in the family who could actually read music, and he had composed a lot of high-brow stuff, including a really modern piece the Columbia orchestra had performed that had real toilets flushing, a piece so innovative it had prompted a fellow composer to physically assault George immediately following the performance.

That Christmas eve, before the plum pudding refused as always to catch fire, George announced that he was engaged to be married to Dorothy, who directed George's church choir. "Very good, George," I said, having encouraged him the spring before to go out with Dorothy and ditch this other girl he was dating at the time, and then we all got misty-eyed, especially the parents, for whom the happy marrying-off of their children was their most cherished goal. Somehow, when you got married, the feeling was you were set for life, off with an eternal smile into the glowing sunset, hand-in-hand, as at the end of an old movie, and the parents would never have to worry again about whether anyone was doing anything for your birthday. George basked in the spotlight for a change while Spencer and I congratulated him on his happiness— believing, though we would never have admitted it, what the parents believed—and made a joke thanking him for taking

69

the pressure to get married off the rest of us. My father said, shaking his head with emotion, that it was one of the happiest days of his life, and my mother, fluttering with excitement, immediately started making plans for the engagement party, announcing, as she eyed with impatience the table set ahead for Christmas dinner, that she was reserving the dining-room table for the next month for all the various lists of people to invite and things to be done. We were all still feeling blessed and a little schmaltzy the next morning as we gathered under the tree to open Harry's letter.

"'Dear Parents and Siblings,'" my mother read aloud with her perfect enunciation, "'I hereby renounce you unless you join the Fellowship of the Cosmos. Love, Harry.'"

Harry had been living in some hovel in Spanish Harlem in New York that fall, and, when not recording with my flute, working day and night for the Fellowship of the Cosmos—a celestial-psychic cult that called itself a church to avoid taxes —for which he'd had the privilege of paying enormous sums of money in membership fees. He'd been introduced to the group by a boyfriend of my third cousin Lulu Bulkeley, a sixtyish spinster of glamorous intonations and giant, clattering jewelry, who'd left the confines of Boston society years earlier for New York, wintering, however, in Paris, where it was so much *cheaper.* (She took *lovers,* we'd been told in whispers, and indeed the only time I ever met Cousin Lulu she was leaping into the face of a young man and saying, with a great horse laugh, "The doctors at Payne-Whitney told me years ago I was *simply* incurable!") I don't think when Mother asked her to look in on Harry while he was in New York an introduction to the Fellowship was exactly what she had had in mind.

At any rate, the Fellowship of the Cosmos had an ingenious method whereby the more money you paid them, the higher you rose in the organization. Harry had kept us abreast of his progression, with short, enthusiastic phone calls whenever he had a second between making money for the Fellowship and receiving his various promotions, but, I regret to say, his

70

enthusiasm had not been shared by the family. One night that November Harry had breathlessly called us to announce that he had just received his certificate from Lady Meredith Davies, certifying his promotion to stratosphere, second grade.

"Oh," my mother had replied. "I thought you passed that long ago."

On Christmas morning, after listening to Harry's letter, we all just sat there amongst the crumpled papers and ribbons, wishing it were yesterday, and then Mother rose with a sigh and went in to see if the house had caught fire yet from the smoldering turkey, which everyone was roasting that year in brown paper bags.

After dinner I called Harry and yelled at him for hurting the parents, and he kept saying, "I see, I see," in this clipped tone to let me know that I couldn't get to him. The Fellowship of the Cosmos was very big on your getting rid of any bad feelings. They did this by letting you lie flat on a table for three hours with a metal sphere resting on your tummy, and after you did this for a while you were supposed to be "void" of all your unpleasant memories. I think there was also something about leaving your body and remembering you had once been in a dungeon in A.D. 1200. In any case, I got mad at Harry over the phone.

"You'd better come home, Harry, right away," I said in what I hoped was a menacing manner, "or else!"

"I see," said Harry.

"I mean it, Harry, that was a terrible thing you did to the parents," I continued.

"I see," said Harry.

"Are you coming home or not?"

"I see," said Harry, cool as could be, and hung up the phone.

It was around two in the morning when Harry arrived, and I happened to be in the kitchen eating Puffed Rice with Sweet 'n Low, or rather drinking them, pouring the dry cereal into a glass, sprinkling the powdery sweetener on top, and gulping them down. They were tasting particularly good that night, as I had just switched over to them from dry bread. I had recently developed a theory that if you ate only one thing you would lose weight—the idea had just hit me one day when I was weighing myself after a bout with strep throat—and the night before my mother had come down at midnight to find me in my starvation hacking away at a frozen loaf of home-made bread with a butcher's knife.

"You're just like the Roman Empire," she had said, *"in its decline,"* and then off she'd swept up the back stairs, looking as if she were headed to a ball in one of the full-length chiffon dressing gowns my Great-Aunt Elizabeth gave her every Christmas because, as Aunt Elizabeth explained, she didn't believe in giving people anything that they needed.

So I was devouring these Rice Puffs when on the back porch I see Harry, looking like Frankenstein in the snowy night, wearing only a sport jacket, flurries resting on the triangle of his long, frizzy hair like fake snow on a Christmas tree. How I realized he was there I don't know, as he couldn't have knocked with all the instruments under his arms. But I wasn't at all startled; I just heaved a little sigh, as if I had been expecting him at 1:50 A.M. and there he was, ten minutes late, and walked over and opened the door.

"It's about time you got here," I said with a frown, as Harry plunked his wet instrument cases on the kitchen table and opened the refrigerator door. Inside the icebox was some hamburger with a little note on it that said "Please save for Aphro." Scout ate dry Gravy Train but Aphrodite, the pedigree, would eat only cooked hamburger. Harry had once opened the icebox and seen two trays of hamburger, one old and crusty, the other red-fresh, and reaching for the fresh had caused Mother to cry out, "No, no, that's for Aphrodite!" before she'd realized what she was saying.

This time, though, Harry just stood in front of the open icebox staring within until, after about five minutes, he finally closed the door. "I shouldn't have come, I shouldn't have come," he said and began to pace around the kitchen.

"Of course you should have come," I said, still trying to be stern. "You had to come after writing that terrible letter."

"I see," said Harry and, taking out my flute, began to play.

"Harry, listen to me," I insisted, as if I had something terribly important to say when really I was just terrified his music would rouse the parents.

"I can't stay, I'm completely unauthorized to be here, I'll be blacklisted as it is."

"Look," I said, "let me make you something to eat." I wasn't much of a cook—there hadn't been much demand for my Puffed Rice in a glass—but I took the hamburger out and cooked it and put lettuce and tomato and salad dressing on top to make one of Harry's special salad-burgers, and then I made up some tuna, using the lid of the can to chop it up, also a Harry invention, remembering not to drain the oil and adding tons of mayonnaise and garlic salt, and then, just to cover myself, I popped into the oven one of the Loretta Veal Parmigian TV dinners, which had been so popular in our youth. But it turned out to be Scout's big night, because Harry wasn't hungry—he was too busy feeling guilty about coming home to be with his family on Christmas night.

"I've betrayed Lady Meredith Davies," Harry said, "but what's worse is that I've let her down."

"What about letting down the parents?" I interjected, but Harry just shook his head and paced back and forth, fingering the padded keys of his saxophone and sometimes blowing out a riff, but softly so as not to wake the parents.

"She believed in me, she trusted me," Harry moaned during an intermission.

"But, Harry, you haven't even met her. Doesn't she live in Africa or South America or something?" I asked, but nothing I said seemed to make any impact. We talked all night, Harry covering the same basic theme over and over and me attempt-

73

ing in vain to apply logic. Harry didn't make a whole lot of sense—it was like he almost didn't hear me, so possessed was he with his mislaid guilt, but at least he was energized for a change, and somehow it was better than seeing him sluggish and depressed.

Then, around six-thirty, just as we heard the pipes in the parents' bathroom getting going, Harry said, "Dig ya later," and was out the door on his way back to New York, where, I was later called collect to be informed, they made him wear an American flag around his arm for a week, to show everyone who could figure it out that Harry was a traitor.

That April I was accepted by Radcliffe and rejected by Yale. Despite my surge of involvement in extracurricular activities, I had had no business applying to either place, since they generally took only one girl from our school and there were twelve girls ahead of me in my class, drab, bookish types like Mandy Plotz, who, when she got dressed up, stuck a gold bobby pin in the side of her stick-straight pixie. The bookish girls were good at going to school, but they weren't smart enough to get as their guidance counselor Mr. Dupre, who knew the head of admissions at Radcliffe. Mr. Dupre advised me that the main thing to remember on the application was not to say you were political—it was the end of 1968, the year of the first student strikes—and other than that, it didn't much matter what you wrote. The Radcliffe application didn't really have an essay section, just two little white spaces under the questions "How have your personal experiences contributed to your intellectual development?" and "How have your academic experiences contributed to your personal growth?" (The Yale application, on the other hand, had said "essay optional" and then given you three blank pages to fill, as a little hint, and you can probably guess which way I'd gone on that, especially since 1969 was the first year Yale was accepting girls, and mainly, if you read the papers, they seemed to be taking only Russian ballerinas who were also nuclear physicists.) So while Joan Dodge and Mandy Plotz were digging their graves describing how they wanted to help the poor and bring about a world without war, I was writing some convoluted thing about my intellectual development—or was it my personal growth—in which out of the blue I casually let drop the fact that I had been saying that very thing the night before to my first cousin once removed, Charles Greenough, the Pulitzer Prize–winning poet.

I had to work Cousin Charlie into the essay section because, while the form had a place for listing family members who had gone to Harvard, that was only for immediate family members, and it wouldn't have been the greatest idea in the world to put down Harry, who had dropped out of Harvard his sophomore year after marching into the dean of students' office and announcing, disdainfully, that all *he* knew was you didn't see squirrels going around having operations. Also, I wasn't lying, at least not technically. Cousin Charlie had been out to dinner that week—it was the night I made the famous remark "What's for dessert, old ice cream?" just as Mother was rounding the corner with a tray of sleeted-over cartons— and he'd read us his latest poems, while my father dozed on the couch and my mother and I sat politely on the edge of our chairs, not understanding one single word. In high school I was good at explaining the significance of the title *Pride and Prejudice,* but when it came to analyzing poetry, forget it. To this day, put a gun to my head, and I still cannot tell you the difference between the tone of a poem and the mood of the poem.

If my father was a little disappointed I wasn't going to Yale —he had wanted to brag to his Yale friends, whom he hated —Harry, resettled at the old Central Square apartment that spring, was thrilled that I would be at Radcliffe and decided he would go back to Harvard and get his degree. This seemed like a great idea at the time—we couldn't have agreed more, although what Harry was re-enrolling for was not readily apparent. Harry was an avowed anti-intellectual by then and didn't read books anymore and sometimes, when he went on at length about some girl he hadn't even met, it was hard to remember he was the genius of the family and had won first prize at all those high school science fairs.

These days, however, Harry wasn't wasting any brain cells figuring out congruent polygons, not when he could be working them on the subject of the various ways to pick up girls, which seemed to be the only discernible reason for his return to school.

"I can't believe my little sister is going to be a Cliffie," Harry would say, and explain how Cliffies were impossible to meet and how through me all that would change. After Harry had finished recording with Tim Hardin that April and left New York, there'd been no more talk about the Fellowship of the Cosmos, and it was like old times, with me going into Cambridge on Saturdays to clean his apartment. I would make an aisle in the junk on the floor and soak the plates caked with old food while Harry, who would have just gotten up, ate one sizzling hamburger after another straight from the frying pan. Sometimes he would go back to bed for a little nap, then get up and repeat the process. Harry didn't have regular meals but let his stomach be his clock.

We talked forever those Saturday afternoons about how great it would be going to classes together, and how I would wear a sign that would say "I am a virgin and my brother is six-foot-seven," it having been recently decided that it was really cool that I was still a virgin, and how one day we would appear in "newsmakers" together in *Newsweek* ("Famous brother and sister, Harry and Elizabeth Reade, leave movie theater"), although what I was going to be famous about was never quite clear.

Saturday evenings I would go over with Harry to the Casablanca, a bar in Harvard Square where he and Spencer had started playing twice a week. Spencer wore only white now, in honor, I suppose, of his switch from marijuana to the maharishi, a change of life-style that was discernible only in

76

that one respect. Spencer had started meditating the winter before, as had Pony, who, to Spencer's great horror, had divulged his mantra to me. It was very important to get a mantra from an authorized teacher who would select the right mantra for you, Spencer said (although later some newspaper article alleged that mantras had been simply based on age), but I had meditated with Pony's mantra, anyway, and to me it was exactly like getting stoned. In any case, Spencer got very clean in his appearance after he started meditating, and he looked divine, and very well dressed really, in his white baggy pants and shirts from Goodwill, as he sat rangily up on a little platform playing guitar and singing in his pure, sweet voice, while Harry played sax or jazz flute or clarinet, behind. Harry, bearded, his frizzy hair down to his shoulders, was as sloppy as ever, his long skinny legs in dirty jeans and his belly protruding from under a colored T-shirt. But when he played, you forgot everything. You just let him take you down to the bottom of his cavernous soul, then up again, reeling, over the top.

When the set was over, I would sit at the front table and pray that people would clap, which occasionally they did, even though the Casablanca was a loud drinking bar. Sometimes Harry would make me move to another table so that the groupie he was interested in wouldn't think I was his date. Harry was quite keen on groupies, most of whom were not women of towering intellect. I remember one touching his flute and saying, awe shaking her squeaky little voice, "Is it made out of metal?"

"Shsh, shsh!" Harry said to me when I started to laugh.

Spencer, on the other hand, had every female in Cambridge in love with him without needing to lift a finger. His emerald eyes, glistening with woe, had to look up just once from his guitar and flash longingly into the blackness of the audience, and the hearts of women filled. And so they came, Radcliffe girls, models, daughters of senators, law students, dancers, one after another, sometimes two at a time, to sit at the foot of the Casablanca stage and moon possessively at Spencer and his beautiful voice.

"And soon you'll pass oooooon!" he would croon while droplets would gather in their eyes. "And Soon You'll Pass On" was secretly dedicated to Scout, who was deaf and blind by now, and to get him to come to you, you had to pound the floor and then he bumped into a wall anyway. Spencer had written the song the year before, when during every visit he would say good-bye and cry over Scout, but finally he'd given up because he knew the next time he came home, Scout would be there to greet him, running joyfully toward a wall. Most nights I would sit patiently at the Casablanca watching Spencer's girl-of-the-night-before gazing forlornly at his girl-of-the-night-to-be, both of whom would throw me entreating looks and try to enlist me in conversation.

"You must be Lizzie!" they would say when they guessed who I was and then add, significantly, "I'm *Marie*," hoping against hope that Spencer had told me all about them. And I, so mature, as only one can be at eighteen, and so cruel, would bestow upon these transient fans no more than a distant smile, lifting my head away from their pleading faces and toward the stage and my brothers, to whom I would belong forever.

In late April the Wendell Mattress Company informed my father they were moving him to New York to cover Westchester County. As a child of the Depression, my father had always counted himself lucky to have any job at all, and he had worked for Wendell since the end of the Second World War, his loyalty never swerving (to this day I am shocked to find people I know are owners of the hated Sealy mattress), despite the fact the company had never even so much as allowed him three weeks of vacation in a row. My father was fifty-eight that year, and it was mean-spirited of Wendell to move him when he was so near to retiring, but the parents took it, as Harry put it, like lambs unto the slaughter. They invited Mr. Bianca, the young hustler who had jockeyed to take over the

78

territory my father had worked so hard and successfully to build up, to a lovely dinner at home, and talked so much about how great their new house in Westchester was that you knew they despised it. "We must try to look on the good side of all this," my mother ventured one night, but even she, marshaling all the forces of her New England grin-and-bear-itness, was hard put to drum up where the fun was in leaving the friends and town they loved behind.

One Saturday afternoon my father returned from running errands, all choked up, his face puffy and red. "I went into the liquor store," he was barely able to get out, "and Stan said, 'Mr. Reade, we're sure going to miss you!' " and you wanted to die for him then and there. My father couldn't go to a baseball game without a little tear welling in his eye because once, when he was a young boy, he had also gone to a baseball game.

My graduation from high school the following month was less than spectacular. I had few friends and no boyfriend to take me to the senior prom, an event I had publicly scorned for two years as "so establishment," refusing invitations from various brave but misinformed seniors, but which now, with the move from Concord looming, had taken on a nostalgic, irresistible appeal. How much fun it seemed suddenly, instead of infantile, how filled with laughter that would become memories to sneak away from the dance with beers and weave in somebody's father's car to the beach in the summer night. But it was too late, and I was too proud, to convey this drastic change of heart to the few dateless senior boys remaining, and so, with a lame, stupid feeling inside I watched the bustle of prom preparations go on without me.

As for the graduation itself, all I can remember from the actual ceremony is that my cardboard hat blew off in the procession and that when I won the award of one hundred dollars for good citizenship from the Knights of Columbus a little snicker broke out among my classmates. The aloof ways and tragic facial expressions that had marked so much of my high school career had not made me a likely candidate for this honor, but apparently the principal, Mr. Cataloni, who conducted himself more like the foreman of the school than its intellectual leader, had tired of giving out the prizes to all the goody-goody girls, and had reportedly announced in a teachers' meeting, "Let's give the money to that girl I pulled the gun on." This was in reference to the Saturday a few months before, when Mr. Cataloni, after getting wind of a rumble to be staged between some white students and the black kids who were now being bused in from Roxbury, tore into the high school brandishing a pistol, trailed by the Concord police force, and burst in upon me in my little Indian-print miniskirt, using the typewriter in the typing and shorthand classroom for my paper "Otto von Bismarck: Maker of Kings." We had evidently become buddies since then, Mr. Cataloni calling out vociferously to me whenever I was within a mile of him. It seemed we had this little joke going about getting my name right on the diploma.

"Your middle name's Chittenden, isn't it, as in 'Chit-Chit-Chittenden Potato Chips?" he would sing out across a courtyard or down a hallway—referring, I gathered, to some commercial on television—or, simply, "Hey, Chittenden Potato Chips!" causing my Mayflower ancestors to turn in their graves. When I got my high school diploma, after all this, "Elizabeth A. Reade" was inscribed across it, in Mr. Cataloni's bold hand.

I had a knack in those days of choosing as my best, and often sole, woman friend some smart girl who didn't like me, and so it was that I spent that summer on Martha's Vineyard with Rachel Linsenberg, a classmate who wasn't getting along with her mother and consequently had lived at our house all spring, parading around the bite mark her mother had administered to her right shoulder. Rachel's parents were getting divorced and we stayed on the Vineyard with her father, who was one of the genius types in Concord with whom my parents did not have much to do, although once that May, in honor

80

of my friendship with Rachel, my father had invited Mr. Linsenberg to play tennis at the club. Mr. Linsenberg was a flashy player with erratic, smashing strokes, but my father, with his consistent, easy hits, had beat him. "Pat ball," I'd heard Mr. Linsenberg growl as he left the court. Mr. Linsenberg was about as different from my father as you could get, and when Chappaquiddick happened that summer, horrifying the parents, who were more upset by the possibility of adultery than of manslaughter, Mr. Linsenberg said, "Teddy Kennedy just got caught with his pants down, big deal."

In any case, Rachel and I spent July getting tanned and, at my suggestion, eating nothing but Lebanon bread, until one afternoon when we were sitting around with some guys Rachel knew from LRY (LRY stood for Liberal Religious Youth, which is what you could become if you were a Unitarian at age thirteen and go off on coed weekends camping out in caves instead of sitting around with the Episcopal Church curate trying to decide if you could in good conscience get confirmed if you weren't 100 percent sure Christ was divine). "Want to go out and get some Lebanon bread?" I chirped in while Rachel and her tangle-haired crew were sitting on the floor toking up. "Fuck you, Elizabeth," Rachel replied casually, without looking up, and I packed up my things and took the commuter plane back to Boston the next morning.

I arrived home August first, just in time to join the parents glumly watching the movers pack the van, carrying, as if its contents were of great value, a box my mother had marked "Lizzie sixth grade," which included an A plus paper about J. D. Salinger. "A shy and modest man," I had written, obviously lifting the sentence from some book blurb, "Jerome David Salinger shuns society"; "perceptive," commented the teacher, in red pencil. "Still living," I concluded, venturing now to use my own words, "he lives in Connecticut." Then we got in the car and drove the three hours to Bedford Hills, a dead little town an hour and fifteen minutes from New York City, Scout standing the whole way and Aphro wheedling and wee-weeing in Mother's lap, although, my father claimed, Aphrodite's behavior had shown a marked improvement once the possibility of her "not making the trip with the team had been in the air."

I should have been terribly excited about getting to be a bridesmaid in George's wedding and then going off to Radcliffe, but when I arrived at the new house, I got a disoriented, panicky feeling inside that was too lonely to be shared, and instead of talking to the parents I fought with them, fleeing every morning on the train into Manhattan, where I let the crowds push me down the streets and in and out of shops like a great tidal wave.

For two years I had longed to escape the confines of Concord —the corner drugstore where the pharmacist knew everyone's name; the five-and-ten, where I'd bought turtle after turtle, their shells inevitably softening within a week, before they went to their just reward; White's Pond, where my father had dramatically swum out to save Frannie Dangle and me giggling so hard we couldn't get the Sailfish back up; the Armory, where, glassesless, I'd once picked a girl for ladies' choice because she was the same color as Wade O'Sullivan; the old Medical Center, where the blond Dr. Brent never found any cavities ("The Reade children never have any cavities," everybody always said, until Spencer went to camp and the dentist there found twenty-three)—a hometown that now breaks my heart with fond memories, but which then, as I struggled to separate myself from my parents, I bridled against. So when I walked the streets of New York and saw limousines parked next to sleeping vagrants and stands of pornographic magazines, it did not occur to me that I was missing the loveliness and familiarity of Concord, where people were so *nice* (a quality so unimportant when you're young it is not deemed worthy of consideration), where nobody had heard of a bicycle lock and everybody had heard of me. All I knew was that if I plunged stale, melting candy bars into my shrunken stomach, as I hurried along toward no destination, the jitteriness would go away, and instead I would feel hopeless and lost and yearn for the rosy youth of controlled starvation that had been mine my senior year, when every night I would lie in bed with a sense of peace as I felt the new bones appearing on my body one by one.

So, one morning when I was feeling particularly out of control, I took a cab from Grand Central over to see a quack diet doctor that Day, a flaky friend of Rachel's, had heard about. The driver went all the way to an address in Brooklyn before I realized the building I wanted was in the Bronx. To me, they were exactly the same place, and in fact, when I got out at the Bronx, it didn't look a whole lot different from what we'd just left in Brooklyn. It was very sunny and hot and the area wasn't really slummy, just rundown and so quiet it was spooky, and I wished I was not wearing my red Merimekko mini dress with the scoop neck, which had looked so bright and cheery on the streets of Concord, Massachusetts.

Dr. Herman Klinck's office was in one of those not new but not old brick buildings you always see from the highway, row upon row, and thank God in heaven you do not live in. The waiting room was crammed with black women who stared blankly at the gummy linoleum floor. Most of them were pregnant and I had a sudden vision of Dr. Herman Klinck giving quickie abortions in the dim rooms beyond. I heard a man screaming at someone, and a young woman scurried out, and then, sure enough, the good doctor appeared, his high-pitched voice going all oily at the unexpected sight of me. After he led me into his office he made a halfhearted pretense of being a real doctor that was almost endearing, asking me my name—"Beth Chittenden," I answered cleverly—and writing it down on the dirty strip of white paper that ran down the length of the examination table.

"So, you want to gain some weight?" he asked, appraising my one-hundred-pound body.

"Oh, no," I said, the very thought chilling my blood to ice. "No! I want to lose weight!" and added quickly, "I have

83

to dance nude in a Broadway play!" Without batting an eye
Dr. Klinck asked me how much money I'd brought and then
poured into a vial an enormous quantity of blue and yellow
pills.

"Take two, one of each, three times a day and come back
when you need more" was his prescription. Almost as an
afterthought he handed me a little slip of paper that said not
to eat a lot of cakes and candies.

The little pills were great. I took a yellow one, feeling
better the moment it hit my tongue, and had a merry chat
with a terribly friendly girl who was struggling in the stall
next to mine in the Grand Central Terminal ladies room
(which had recently become like a second home to me), peel-
ing off layer after layer of clothes she'd just swiped from
B. Altman's.

"I'm a working girl," she'd explained.

"Oh, where do you work?" I had asked, and then after a
few graphic details I got the picture. *How interesting it is to see
the other side of life,* I reflected somberly as I got on the train,
and immediately struck up a lively conversation with the con-
ductor about exactly what he did all day, which I suddenly
realized I'd always wanted to know.

I was having such a fascinating time that I was sorry when
the train stopped at Bedford Hills. The parents, meeting me
at the station, were astonished by my high spirits but, un-
willing to look a gift horse in the mouth, soon joined me in
an animated discussion of my day, minus the more crucial
details. I stayed up all that night reorganizing my trunk of
miniskirts and had a grand old time, but the next day I was a
little cranky, so I decided to pack away the pills for an emer-
gency later in life, if, for instance, I gained a pound. For
twelve dollars I'd gotten enough diet pills to last a century, so
I poured a bunch into a manila envelope and sent them off to
Day at Bennington. She wrote me later that she had blithely
opened the envelope during her freshman picnic, the bright
capsules spilling out onto the ground between her and the

dean of students, but of course at Bennington people were too busy being ethereal to notice.

But the panic had vanished, and on the morning of George's wedding I felt really great as I looked in the mirror and thought, *Well, this is the best you are ever going to get.* I was thin and tanned and it was a good, humidity-free day for my strawberry-blond hair, which fell fashionably down the sides of my face like a pair of curtains. Just as you were supposed to have straight hair, mine had turned curly and I slept with it tightly wrapped around my head, the tipless bobby pins knifing my scalp, and that morning I had awoken with joy and a throbbing headache to discover the turban still snugly in place.

As a bridesmaid, I got to wear a long peach dress, which reminded me of the one in a portrait of my Great-Aunt Elizabeth as a bridesmaid that hung next to my mother's dressing table. I think she was forty-five in the picture, though she looks twenty-five—her secret, she always said, was to stay in bed five days every month. Aunt Elizabeth was my godmother and she and I liked to keep up the illusion that life was a fairy tale and we were both princesses, even during that time of rebellion when I had refused to let her give me the coming-out party we'd talked of for years, due to the moral grounds one had in 1969 but can't quite articulate now.

Aunt Elizabeth told me later she never took her eyes off me at the wedding, not so much as glancing at the bride, which might have been a bad call, seeing as I keeled over in a dead faint halfway through the ceremony. George's fiancée, Dorothy—a big, tall girl with black slanted glasses—had recently become religious, in rather a modern, though Presbyterian, way ("The motto of our prayer group is 'No more Mr. Nice Guy,'" she remarked at dinner the night before), and the entire wedding party had to remain standing through the hour-long ceremony, in which every time you looked you were singing some hymn you didn't know the tune, or the words, to. The wedding party hadn't been given hymnals and just after the fourth verse was over and you thought, *At last, at last, please God let it be over,* old Dorothy would start in enthusiastically on verse five, her operatic voice booming out over the church. Then all these prayer group friends of hers had to go up and read lessons from the Bible, while we bridesmaids stood there, swaying in our peach heels. "And so, He spake, let the lame man rise," said a gangly girl with great significance, after which they had to drag my lifeless body straight down the center aisle of the church and out to the steps before I came to.

The reception, however, was great. We loved Dorothy's family, who knew how to have a good time, meaning they drank, and we all got high on champagne, only Harry never came down.

Chapter Seven

Harry was a manic-depressive, of course, as was my mother, as were so many members of my mother's family, including Charlie Greenough, who had a breakdown each year of his adult life, generally following the Thanksgiving get-together at Great-Aunt Elizabeth's weekend farm. Every November Charlie would fly in for Great-Aunt Elizabeth's turkey dinner, and every November he would look at me vaguely from behind his wild hair and say, "Haven't you grown taller or something?" which frankly didn't seem so brilliant to me, and then he would sit at the table gazing off into the distance on account of always being seated next to Cousin Dee Dee, who was writing a book in French about her visions of Marie Antoinette at Versailles. Cousin Dee Dee herself had been a manic-depressive, I found out later, having flipped out for the first time at age twenty-eight and, after the hysterectomy they gave her (as they did in those days, assuming the problem was female), she had continued to flip out every nine months for the next twenty years, until her beloved husband, who had been so wonderful about it all, died, and then she never had another breakdown. Anyway, Cousin Charlie never said much of anything at Thanksgiving, but then it didn't really matter what Charlie said once he'd won the Pulitzer. "Charlie's a genius, you know," Great-Aunt Elizabeth would whisper confidentially to you after Charlie murmured some non sequitur, while all Spencer and Harry ever got from her on these occasions was "Are you normal yet?" At any rate, after dinner Charlie would be out there with the rest of us in borrowed galoshes, chilled to the bone as we tramped in the rain to the various barns to look, not without envy, at Uncle Win's prize cows, who lived in warm, softly lit, immaculate stalls with pedigrees neatly hung above, and then, bang, one week later he'd be locked up in the nut house crazy as a loon. I was told at the time that Charlie checked himself into Brookhill whenever he needed a rest.

Manic depression was never exactly explained to us in our youth—there was no paperback book on it like the one my father slipped under my brothers' doors at a certain age, called *The Facts of Life,* with the boy and the girl on its cover sharing a soda with two straws—but it was a term we grew up with, bandied about, applied here and there, sometimes casually, sometimes with a hushed drama, to this relative or that, applied even to Mother, whose one and only breakdown we could neither visualize, having been sheltered from it, nor, judging from the normality of a motherhood that insisted on a green with every meal and only one hour of TV a day, truly believe. Somehow manic depression was too romantic for our ordinary kind of mother, and early on we erased the fact of her previous breakdown from our minds. Even when Harry broke down for the first time, the rest of us were kept at enough of a distance from it that flipping out could look, two years down the line, like a viable way to go for Spencer, miserable and lost at age eighteen, and one that might finally put him on a par with Charlie and Harry, the family geniuses. When Spencer couldn't seem to really go crazy, he'd felt not relief but failure. "I'm just not smart enough to go nuts," he'd confessed to me one afternoon, after Cousin Charlie, who was staying in an-

88

other wing at Brookhill, had drifted absently by the basketball court to murmur a distracted hello.

None of us could help but believe that manic depression was connected to being a genius, except for my mother, who would say, "What about Great-Aunt Baby Apwell?" (whenever I went to the symphony with Great-Aunt Elizabeth she would wave at this ninety-nine-year-old woman, creeping to her front row seat on the arm of her equally ancient chauffeur, and cry out, "Look, it's Baby Apwell!"), who, when she got high, only got more and more boring until nobody paid her any attention and she had to put herself away.

As for my mother's own experience, it was upon my birth that, overjoyed at finally being delivered of a girl after three boys, she promptly went into a mental hospital for two years. Actually, Mother said, it took a week before anyone noticed she was high. All the relatives just sat there chatting away and admiring my smashed-in little face, while Mother piped in from time to time about being God or something until my Grandfather Chittenden turned to my father and said, "Don't you think Charlotte's a little inky-binky?" and that was that.

How my father dealt with all this I do not know. Coming from his nice Baltimore family he hadn't the benefit of a long psychotic heritage to fall back on and probably imagined a future of lunatic asylums and straitjackets, his sole point of reference being the movie *The Snake Pit*—but then, my father had a strong survival instinct that clicked on in times of trouble and allowed him to suddenly start thinking out the chords of "Ain't Misbehavin'."

All I know is that I was too young to remember any of it. Evidently we had a great housekeeper, paid for by the grandparents, and George, who was seven, got suspended from school after threatening to throw an eraser at his teacher (my father burst into tears when he went to speak to the principal, and took George to a shrink, who only told him, "George is fine; I'd watch out for that second son of yours"); and Harry, who was five, suddenly became perfect in every way, as if it

89

had been his imperfection that had sent Mother to the hospital; and Spencer, who was three, became my protector; and I, they say, when I learned to sit, sat bolt upright in the lap of anyone who would rock me; and my father went to people's houses for dinner every night and played a lot of squash and a lot of banjo and gave up trying to set the world on fire at the Wendell Mattress Company. And then, after a couple of years, my mother came home and has been as normal as can be ever since.

The point is, half the people in my mother's family are manic-depressive and the other half are screwed up about it, and sometimes it is hard to tell who is what and whether people are being crazy or just normal. Is my Cousin Westy crazy when he decides to jog from Louisiana to Canada, eating out of garbage cans, not a penny in his pocket? No, he has a great time, comes back, starts a computer company, gets married, and has four kids. Is my Aunt Peaches crazy when she shows her psychiatrist pictures of the raccoon she used to feed, dead these thirty-five years, or my Great-Aunt Theodora, who, when her husband is presented a gift at a Harvard fund-raiser, cries out, as he opens it before hundreds, "Save the paper!" Was Harry crazy that night at Uncle Hank's house after the wedding when he kept talking a mile a minute about the fate of the universe while the rest of us lay on couches with horrible hangovers?

"Harry, relax," said Spencer, who usually never drank but had popped champagne corks at cars all the way to Westport, as he gently lifted his head to light a cigarette, and then the phone rang.

"Your call to the United Nations has gone through, sir," the operator informed Uncle Hank, who, without missing a beat, passed the phone to Harry. Uncle Hank was a high-powered type who ran a hundred newspapers and had absolutely no time for anything (generally he'd be limoed in for family weddings and have to leave before the reception), except when it came to his adopted daughter, who at one point housed in their Washington apartment fifty pets for whose birthday parties Uncle Hank would interrrupt board meetings in order to attend, and Harry, whom, for some reason, Uncle Hank adored, partly because Harry was so tall.

Harry went with an official air to take the call in the next room, and he was still squirreled away an hour later when the rest of us cousins dragged ourselves to bed. Of course I should have realized that Harry was crazy then and there, but in those days everybody talked about the fate of the universe, and then, Harry was having such a good time, for a change.

It had been such a great day, too, all of us dressed to kill, even the brothers in cut-aways, and my father throwing me a wink at the reception as he strummed away in the band, where he and Spencer and Harry were sitting in, and Harry catching the garter off Dorothy's leg, and a stream of us running to spray the getaway car with shaving cream—a wedding day just like normal families were supposed to have. And George, in the center of the family for this precious moment in his life, getting his picture taken with everybody's arm around him, including Harry's, looking so content, even though, in the end, even on his wedding day George would be upstaged by Harry—although, of course, it was only in retrospect that this day became the day Harry began going nuts. At the time we were all too determined to notice only how happy we were.

So, when I went back to Westchester the following morning, my brain was filled only with wondering how to make the time pass until that Saturday, when I was due up at Radcliffe. The hours dragged for me in Bedford Hills that week as I stood gazing at myself and my new clothes in the mirror every two seconds, but not for Harry, it turned out, who was back in Cambridge treating everyone royally. Somehow he managed to convince the Cambridge Cooperative Bank to give him a Mastercharge, even though he didn't have an account there, or a dime to his name, and he spent the week arranging private dinner parties for William and Spencer and my cousin Art at Luttinger's, an old, very expensive restaurant that featured disagreeable gentleman waiters. The sky was the limit at Harry's banquets, and Harry kept ordering up rounds of escargot while telling the group that they had been chosen to save the world from Communism. It was no accident, Harry explained, that both Art and William were members of SDS (Art, in fact, had been president of Harvard's SDS chapter the year before and had, for some reason, worn a fire extinguisher under his gown at his graduation that spring.) William, who had always known how to live no matter what his politics—it was during this period that he began to pay his Mastercharge bill with his Diner's Club card—told me later that the little dinners were hard to resist, given Harry's less than open-handed history, and were really rather pleasant affairs, except when Harry did things like fire the waiter or pull the phone out of the wall. He had had the phone installed at great expense in order to keep in close touch with the recording you could call to get the exact time. He would stand there between courses, the receiver cradled on his shoulder, his eyes glued to his watch.

"When the time on the phone synchronizes with the time on this watch," Harry had informed his guests tersely, "the money will come in."

Meanwhile the parents and I were just going along our merry way—suddenly remembering we'd forgotten to pack me toothpaste or shampoo, and frantically dashing out, as if these commodities could never be found again anywhere but at the Drug Barn in Mount Kisco—until that Friday, when Harry called to inform us he was about to disclose his plans for saving the universe. We threw my trunk of miniskirts and short sweaters into the mustard-colored Subaru and drove up to Cambridge a day early.

It was almost midnight when we pulled up to the address Harry had given us—a recording studio off some alley in the

92

South End—and evidently we were late, for there, already standing on the curb, were Spencer, William, Art, and Uncle Hank, who had just driven his own car at a hundred miles per hour in from Manhattan, and at their feet, smoking away on a cigarette as if her life depended upon it, a girl nobody knew, who had happened to be sleeping with Spencer when he'd gotten the call about saving the universe. The parents and I got out of the car and said "Hi!" in this kind of surprised way, as if what a coincidence to run into one another at twelve midnight in an alley next to the Combat Zone, and then everyone started talking all at once, with William, Art, and Spencer filling us in on the events of the past week.

Somehow, it was felt, the sudden sight of the parents at this hour and place would alarm Harry and alert him that something was up, so the plan was for them and Uncle Hank to hide around the corner, while the rest of us were to go into the studio, act real natural, and then kidnap Harry and take him to the Boston Mental Rehabilitation Center. The reason we were taking him to Boston Rehab, which was a public institution, was that there was no way the parents could afford another stint at Brookhill, which was then going for a grand a week. Also, my mother had some vague idea that going to Boston Rehab might teach Harry some responsibility, although under the circumstances this seemed a bit optimistic.

The moment that Art, William, Spencer, and I walked through the door into the lobby we felt awful pretending we'd just happened to drop by to listen to the music and oh, by the way, please tell Harry to come out and say hello when he got a chance. We could hear Harry in the room beyond wailing away on the sax, wild and brilliant. Then the music stopped and Harry came out.

He was waving a sheaf of papers, which, he informed us, were his plans to rescue the world, and he began to pace up and down, puffing on a cigarette with a worried air.

"I've got to get to the UN tonight, or else," Harry said, looking very handsome and forceful, I must say, in his new

93

double-breasted sport jacket, holding himself up to his full six-foot-seven inches in height. He hadn't looked so good in years, if you want to know the truth.

"Lady Meredith Davies's got enough to do dealing with the universe, so she's put me in charge of earth," Harry said with a large sigh, the burden of it seeming to fall heavily onto his shoulders. He looked us over carefully, assessing our limited capabilities realistically, resignedly, but not without a courageous hopefulness. "And now," he continued, with a frown, "I must delegate the tasks."

"Harry, you are crazy and we are taking you to the hospital," I said in a quiet, even voice, as if I'd been kidnapping crazy people all my life; maybe I was genetically predisposed —it would make sense.

"You fucking hunk of meat!" Harry replied.

"Come on, Harry," I said, and reached my arm up over his shoulder. For all his size and passion, I was never to be afraid of Harry when he was crazy. He put his arm around me for an instant, and then, as if he'd just remembered, he began a halfhearted struggle that was probably pretty believable if you weren't up close, and we all herded him out to Art's bright red SDS van.

"They nailed Christ to the cross!" Harry screamed as a warning from time to time, as we drove the van around in circles, pretending we were going to the UN, where Harry had called a special Security Council meeting, and the girl nobody knew whispered to me, "What if he's right?"

When we got to the hospital, we were all pretty cool— William had led the kidnap team years before, at Harry's first breakdown, and Art had a twin brother crazy as the night was long—and then the parents materialized, like Ozzie and Harriet out of the blue, along with Uncle Hank, and everything went very fast, with Harry barking out orders and gesticulating magnificently, and the last thing I remember is Harry writing down on the admittance form, "Address: Heaven," and they took him away.

94

I was kind of exhilarated after all this, and my father and I decided to go out after we dropped Mother off at the hotel. It was about two AM when we parked the car in Harvard Square, and we were hungry as can be. So we went over to Hayes-Bickford, a cafeteria-type place that was open all night. The restaurant was filled with street people who came up to guess our signs and drunk Harvard clubbies in tuxedos ordering eggs and making remarks. We bought a couple of triangles of cold apple pie, which was the first solid food I'd eaten in front of my father in a year, and sat down at a table that looked out onto the Square, which was hopping with panhandlers and musicians and one guy who drew your picture on the sidewalk, and it was a good thing he drew it on the sidewalk because it was not something you needed to take home. I was still feeling excited and, for some reason, really great, and I talked to my father all about how I couldn't wait to fall in love at Harvard that fall, and my father talked to me about his college flame, Miriam Cobb, and how the funny thing was, the guy she'd ended up marrying hadn't turned out to be a wheel at all. My father is very happy with my mother, I should mention. It's just that he is a southern boy and very dreamy.

Chapter Eight

"Some people get more out of Harvard than others," Dean Codgeman solemnly told the freshman class that Monday morning in Sanders Theatre, and 1,550 of us thought, *How true, how true*, with a shake of our heads, as we stole looks at one another, thinking with a tremble, *These, too, have that indefinable thing, that something special that makes them Harvard men*. At the end of his speech the dean gestured, and, like children of the Lord, we rose as one and, crying with full heart, sang the Harvard Song. The assembly over, we poured out of the theater into Harvard Yard, dazzling in the September sun, and spilled into Harvard Square.

We continued on into the Harvard Coop, passing the Crimson sweatshirts and T-shirts with a smug air, too cool to buy them but proud down deep, and journeyed up to the third floor to receive our Harvard Coop card, which allowed us, as students, the privilege of charging books, toothpaste, and pantyhose at 18 percent interest. "My roommate and I have the same taste in posters!" announced one eager boy waiting in line, as equally fascinating conversations pierced the air, often containing, as if by chance, the mention of college board scores.

A hundred times I had walked through Harvard Square, but now I was a part of it, and I marched down the streets and into the shops with a proprietary air, buying, with my shiny new Coop card an Indian-print bedspread to brighten my room and, to add meaning, a black-and-white poster of a figure screaming in a tunnel with his hands over his ears, which I thought very original until I later saw it on the walls of about half the freshman class. The streets were thronged with pamphleteers in dirty jeans and waist-length hair—members of cults, bums, ragamuffins all, but in those days commanding respect. I took every pamphlet handed me, with plans to conscientiously study them later in my room, except for the one from the guy from the Fellowship of the Cosmos, with whom I had a lengthy, spirited argument of no impact.

One bum on Brattle Street I recognized from an acting class I'd taken years before. I knew for a fact his parents were worth millions, but there he stood, plain and simply begging in Harvard Square. He was a short, unattractive guy who had been smart as a whip and almost bald at twelve. "Let me take you into my office," he said, after coming up to hug me, and swung me into the Harvard Trust. I gave him a dollar, but not out of pity—there seemed something almost noble about panhandling, I couldn't exactly put my finger on it. On another corner stood a group of Hare Krishna, chanting and ringing bells in front of the subway kiosk, as they would, in rain or shine, the entire time I was at Radcliffe, wearing lovely saris like the ones the mothers in Concord wore the summer they all took trips to the Far East, having used up Europe.

I probably should have been depressed, what with throwing my brother in a loony bin the first day at college, but to tell you the truth, it kind of slipped my mind. In and out of lecture halls I drifted that September, each day in a new little size six outfit, my freshly washed hair long and gleaming, my face turned sunnily upon a thousand men. The problem was, the only guys who came up to you were the clean-cut jerks who would ask, "What course are *you* taking?" as if anyone could give a hoot.

For years I had wanted only to make Harry happy, and why, now that the worst had happened, I could think only about falling in love, I cannot say. But whatever the reason, my mind wasn't on Harry; it hadn't been even the morning after the kidnapping, when I'd turned to the parents, as they paused for breath after depositing the last trunk in my room at Radcliffe, and said, brightly, "Well, I guess it's time for you to be shoving off!" and then actually kissed them in the hopes this uncharacteristic display of affection might take the place of an hour's chitchat and send them on their way. My roommate had already arrived but gone off somewhere, and I wanted to take this time to be alone in my room in Daniels, the new dorm at Radcliffe, alone with its sheetrocked, characterless walls and clean linoleum floor, which I loved as I have never loved anything modern since.

My roommate, Alison, turned out to be a handsome girl from a wealthy, no-nonsense midwestern family. She wore jeans and baggy men's shirts, and later confessed that, upon looking in my closet and seeing the row upon row of precious little skirts, she'd figured I was a real jerk. Nevertheless we liked each other right off and sat up most of the nights that first week, drinking Tab and smoking cigarettes, *Abbey Road* blaring out the opened windows. Alison told me an awful story about how she had almost been raped that summer, by some guys who picked her up in a van or something. I don't remember many of the details because the whole time I spent trying to steer the conversation toward the important topic of when we could expect to have boyfriends. Radcliffe had twenty-three-hour visitation rights and you got to feeling pretty embarrassed if you weren't letting some foggy guy out your bedroom door in the morning. The "we" was kind of a royal we, as Alison wasn't technically looking for a boyfriend, because she had what my parents would have called "a heavy beau" back in Saint Louis, whereas I had not had a date for over a year, a fact that had nearly driven my father to the grave.

At first I sought to remedy this plight by sitting around every night at Hilles, the brand new library on the Radcliffe campus. Hilles was very plush, with deep velour armchairs and large picture windows, and beautiful guys with long, stringy hair were bending over books wherever you looked. I would have married any of them on the spot, but I wasn't sure how to get their attention, and I didn't have the concentration even to pretend to study. I had been really good at studying in high school, but the whole time at college I couldn't get through a single page in a book to save my soul. I'd sit up straight and alert at my desk and start to read about how the American Revolution wasn't fought because of high ideals but actually because of some economic trend of the masses, which they'd illustrate for you with a dreary, tiny-print graph, and the next thing I knew, there I'd be face-down on the shiny, cool text, sleeping away as if there were no tomorrow.

I should mention that never, not for a minute, did I have any intention of doing one lick of work at Harvard. Brilliantly had I discussed the origins of totalitarianism with my Radcliffe interviewer, hotly disputing the theories of Hannah Arendt, the whole time thinking about that boy-girl ratio of four to one. Anyway, Harvard was pretty hard to flunk out of if you took the right courses—they had this theory that once you were in you were in, as opposed to Yale, which not only expected you to read the books but had the gall to expect you to go to the lectures. William had given me advice: "Know nothing and when you sit down to write the exam your mind will be wondrously clear." William was in his second year at Harvard Law School, though mainly what he did was sip red wine and go to strident SDS meetings, where everybody shouted at everybody else about issues upon which they seemed to be in total agreement. I went with William to a meeting once that September, but all the guys had short hair, so what was the point?

Since I wasn't exactly getting near the altar catching up on my sleep at Hilles, I decided the thing to do was to get involved in some kind of activity where the deep, suffering types would be. So I picked the freshman play. The freshman play was called *The People vs. Leech* and had one major role, Leech, and then everyone else got placed in these two mobs that yelled at each other the whole time, improvising mean things to say. It was an experimental thing and you didn't even have to try out—you were guaranteed a part.

The first rehearsal was on Sunday night in early October, and I was in a great mood, even though I'd spent a sinking afternoon visiting Harry at Boston Mental Rehab. My mother had come up from Westchester—my father had had to stay home to take Aphro, who had eaten an entire chicken, bones and all, to the vet—and we'd sat with Harry in the small overheated area they called the "day room" (you never got to see the "night room," where everyone slept, row upon row of metal beds), with the birds chirping in cages and the fat woman selling candy bars at the door and the drugged-up patients walking around in circles looking for places to sit. It was like a popular Greyhound bus station late at night, even down to having the guy standing around with the nervous twitch. I found out later that this was the twitch you got after so many months of taking Thorazine, the drug mental hospitals now used instead of straitjackets, a drug that had once been used as an insecticide. One young girl walked 'round and 'round the room keeping track of each revolution. "One hundred fourteen," she'd say in a dull, hopeless voice, and the next thing you knew, you started to root for her. Mother and I did most of the talking while Harry just sat there, too drugged up to wash his face or light a cigarette, and then we got in the Subaru and drove to Radcliffe.

The whole way back I kept telling my mother that I just knew I was going to fall in love that night, and by the time

101

we got up to my dorm room I think both of us were convinced. She sat perkily in my white room, on the Indian bedspread, underneath the poster of the guy screaming in the tunnel, and I rocked in my rocking chair smoking cigarettes and getting all excited and trembly about my premonition and getting her all excited and trembly, too. My mother and I had a way of running full force with a ridiculous idea when there was nothing to be done about reality, and in this silly but genuine manner, we comforted each other about Harry.

When I got to the Loeb Drama Center that night in my sweater and cut-off corduroys, I found all these Radcliffe girls in old clothes looking around expectantly, not a Leech in sight, and I must say, things looked pretty dim. The director, a Professor Leviten, got us all on the floor and told us in a deep, lulling voice to try to feel heavy, heavy, hea-vy. Just as we were sink-ing, sink-ing into the cool linoleum, all of a sudden a boy came rushing in, which I knew because I cheated and crooked an eye open. He was skinny and tall, his face ashen, his hair long and dirty—he looked like he had just gotten over the flu—and my spirits soared.

This was Richard Townsend, with whom I was to be so violently in love, but I suppose it could well have been any one of a hundred guys. My theory on love is that it is all timing. With the parents in Westchester and Harry in Boston Rehab, I was, beneath all my excitement, desperately lonely and desperate to escape, and Richard was the first decent prospect to come within reach. I was like those baby ducks in tests who open their eyes at birth and the first thing they see is a football, which they follow around for the rest of their lives. Except that I'm lying, and I might as well admit that there was something wonderful about Richard, so that even when he looked intently at you and said, in that husky voice, something asinine like "I recognize your eyes," which would have sent my brothers and William and I guess most men into gales of laughter, you didn't care, you were on Richard's side,

102

you gladly gave him a dispensation to say anything without being a jerk, and you got weak in the knees, even though you knew the instant he said it that he'd said it before and he'd say it again to another girl before the night was out. It was Richard's total, unabashed sincerity when he uttered these cringingly poetical remarks that allowed you to believe what you wanted to believe, what made it all so much easier—that love was magic and conquered all. And I cannot even say that if I saw Richard again, as he was at that moment with that mop of hair and those deep-blue melancholy eyes that looked right at you, as only actors are able to do without getting all embarrassed, that, even knowing everything that I know now, I would not feel what I felt then at the sight of him.

Somewhere in the distance I heard Leviten rumbling on about how Richard Townsend was a sophomore and the student director of *The People vs. Leech,* and then Richard, as he took over from Leviten on the sinking, sinking of us girls.

"Let your body dissolve into the floor, becoming with it as one," he said in a quiet, resonant, authoritative voice that crept down my spine as it cuddled into the linoleum, comfy as could be. We lay pretending we were the floor for a while and then my new love got us up to do the "trusting exercise," herding us into a close circle that was supposed to be a huddle, except we were girls and didn't know how to do it. I felt very relaxed and threw Richard what I thought was a penetrating look. I had a kind of power, when the mood hit me—a mood that had, unfortunately, been conspicuously absent for a year —and when it came on, no matter what I was wearing or how fat I was, I could get just about any boy in sight, even guys I had no business trying for. I wasn't sure whether Richard had noticed me, but when he picked me to be the body that stood in the middle of the group and flung itself backward, trusting, trusting the others to catch me before I crashed to the floor breaking my back in two, I knew everything was going to work out just fine. I let my eyes close and abandoned myself

103

to the blackness of the fall, letting go of everything that had been so tight for years and waiting to feel Richard's arms, among all the others that caught me.

Exercise after exercise we floated through, and by ten o'clock I don't know if any of us could have acted our way out of a paper bag, but we sure were peaceful; it was like being on drugs. In those days, you were either on drugs or trying to act like you were. I watched Richard take out a red Bic pen and write down all our names and phone numbers.

"I have a pen just like that," I said, for by now, anything went.

"Can I walk you home?" Richard said straight through me, and I said sure.

We spoke softly as we walked the half mile to Radcliffe—somehow I knew the way to be with Richard was soft and serious—and when we got to the dorm my heart took a leap of daring and I asked, "Want to come up?" rather casually, considering Alison was away for the weekend and we would be alone in a room with beds, and up we went.

Richard Townsend had black eyebrows and a hawk nose and a soft, expressive face, but what really did the trick were those eyes, which could be so intense one moment and so sweet the next and which were always so direct you didn't have much choice but to fall back on the bed. But we didn't fall back on the bed for hours that first night; we sat cross-legged on it facing each other, talking and talking till it was beginning to get light outside and my head was beginning to ache from all the soulful staring, when finally Richard said, "Let's do the exercise where you close your eyes and touch the other person's face," which sounds a bit sneaky, but he managed to pull it off, and anyway, I didn't care, because at last I was feeling his gentle hands on my face, and my neck, and then all over the place, until nothing else in the world had ever mattered.

"It takes so long to get to know a person's body," Richard murmured thrillingly, promising a million brilliant tomorrows, and I said, "I know what you mean," not knowing at all what he meant, and thinking, *I guess this is going to be the big time,* though things remained at the clothed stage. But we were eighteen and nineteen, and so, even fully dressed, it was eight in the morning before we could pull ourselves apart, and then I snuck Richard out the front door of the dorm, feeling very cool and with it.

"See you," he said burningly, holding my chin with the tip of his hand.

"Same here," I whispered happily, if stupidly, as Richard drew his fingers lyrically away in the air and turned to leave.

Richard came back the next evening, his thick brown hair clean and shiny, with a streak of white in it. He had been painting the walls of poor people's houses in Roxbury, a part of some program they had at Harvard. Richard was always getting fervently involved in programs, I was to learn, though his ardor never lasted. My face grew pink to see him there, in person, at my door, so beautiful and accessible, and he stood smiling and silently taking me in, and then he presented me with an onion and an orange.

"Oh," I said, a bit taken aback, even in those days of symbolism. "Thank you."

"I just wanted to see what you would do with them," he said meaningfully. Richard was always testing one for deepness. Richard was very deep—I mean I guess he was deep, I don't really know, as I am shallow as a puddle. At the time, though, I hadn't given up on my quest to be deep, and would gladly have stood in front of a firing squad if it would have made me so, and Richard's moist eyes and hushed voice touched me and gave me hope. *What a big heart he has,* I thought, touching the oil-based paint in his hair, although later I was to wish his heart was just a teensie bit smaller with a weensie bit less room in it for all the others.

That October, while Richard was seeing me every day and showering me with onions, he was wrapping up a long romance with a grave little black-haired girl named Sophie Riolo. Richard had met Sophie the fall before in a freshman

105

acting seminar, and they'd had an intense, caring relationship the entire year, with a little break during spring vacation when Sophie had gone home to visit her widowed mother and Richard had had a dramatic, fraught-with-meaning affair with Francie Kaplan, a stocky, worldly girl in her junior year. Things were very serious for a couple of days, including wrenching scenes, in the dining hall and in front of the dorm, of Francie breaking up with her lawyer fiancé, who'd flown in from New York for the occasion, but when Sophie came back from vacation, Richard decided Francie had been a mistake. "Francine, this is wrong," I can hear him saying nobly at the very last second of spring vacation.

Coincidentally, Francie Kaplan was my "big sister," and I will never forget the look on her face when she met up with me and Richard Townsend in the elevator in Daniels.

"Francie, this is Richard," I said in the pride of young love, not knowing, of course, anything of their romance, and Richard turned his dark-blue gaze upon her, keeping it there until the elevator stopped, setting her back, I figure, about six months.

As for Sophie, the first day of college that fall, she had run into Richard's room and kissed him awake, and Richard had announced he didn't love her anymore, and Sophie had announced she thought she might have leukemia. The whole time Richard was plying me with sensuous looks, they were doing tests on Sophie Riolo to see if she was going to die. It was not a wonderful fall for Sophie; she told me later (there being a later, it turning out she was only anemic) how she first saw me standing on the steps of William James Hall, glistening in the sunlight in my red sweater, white skirt, and yellow maryjane shoes, and how her heart sank as she saw Richard running up the steps toward me like a billy goat. Richard was a rock climber and was always fording imaginary streams on the way to the movies or scampering up the roofs of Harvard at night to keep in shape. I knew, of course, something about Sophie maybe dying and all, as she ate in my dining hall, and I would often see her wan face in the food line; but I was too desperately in love and I couldn't bring myself to think about anything else. None of it was real, none of it mattered—all that mattered was being with Richard Townsend.

There was no longer any reason to go to classes now that I had Richard. In the mornings I would wash my hair, and around two I would take the freshly painted Red Line subway over to Park Street, in Boston, then board the grimy North Avenue-Broadway, which bumped over broken streets, dreary stop after stop, through the old mill district, past the trolley junkyard to the treeless outskirts of the city where Boston Rehab was, so that by the time I got there, I felt so depressed I almost fit in. It was still a big effort for Harry to talk, but at least he made sense when he did, not like the sweet Italian guy who stood smiling against the wall chirping "airport" from time to time, though I suppose you could make a case that he was happier. Mainly Harry and I would sit there pretty quietly in the bright light of the day room, me wondering when Richard would find that Tootsie Pop I'd stuck in the middle of his book, until I would begin to talk about how great Richard was, which was a bit hard to articulate, I have to admit, and hope from a flicker of his face that Harry was interested. Sometimes we would play a slow game of gin rummy while we waited for a three-cushioned couch. The day room had both two-cushioned and three-cushioned plastic yellow couches and the big thing was to get a three-cushioner, Harry said, so you could lie down. People would sit there kind of casual and all until someone got up to go to the bathroom, and then they'd jump up and dash over, in a Thorazine kind of way, to grab the vacated three-cushioned couch.

In the late afternoon I would go over to Richard's room in Adams House and sit with him through the evenings while he tried to study. Richard was stuck in the living room of a two-bedroom suite he shared with two juniors who were math

107

majors, and he had fashioned a tent out of sheets that extended over his bed and desk, and under which we had a little life going as we fiercely pretended the juniors weren't walking around the living room talking about pi *r* squared or playing awful comedy records. Richard and I spent every night under this tent, and while we didn't sleep together in the technical sense, the sex and so forth was just the greatest and every night I knew I would be Richard's forever and forever until the end of time. My virginity seemed a silly thing now, in light of such momentous feelings, and I wanted so to give it up, but Richard felt that it was important that we both be in love with each other first.

Our most amorous times occurred when Richard had a test the next day or a paper due and he would wake me up at two in the morning to listen to a tape recording of the entry door opening or some poem he'd just written about my hands. Richard was big on writing poems, often leaving them written on napkins as tips when we went to the Pewter Pot for a muffin or something, which I thought adorable, although I'm not so sure the waitresses would have agreed. His poetry was very serious and didn't make any sense, but he looked awfully cute when he read it to you, gesturing and frowning in his Shakespearean way. The problem with it was, you really had to be there, and when his family asked him to write a little something for the yearly Christmas letter, his "Their souls merging to create a faceless void, moving, moving" looked pretty funny next to his sister's story about how she'd finally found her contact lens on the bathroom scale.

During the weekends Richard and I were together every minute, drifting out for breakfast on the fire escape by late morning, and rolling over to Harvard Stadium in the afternoon so Richard could run up and down the stadium steps, while I sat there as lit-up in my pride as the blue sky and red leaves surrounding us. One Saturday we took a little holiday from Richard's step-practicing to go over to Morgan Memorial, where I bought him a fourteen-dollar suit dating back to the forties so that he would have something to wear to dinner at Great-Aunt Elizabeth's on Beacon Street.

"Look how nicely Richard's jacket hangs, Win," Great-Aunt Elizabeth had said as we sat in her beautiful living room, which was cozy because of her famous trick of making sure each room had one shabby thing in it, and in truth Richard looked more handsome in the incongruity of the dark-blue pin stripe suit than ever I had imagined. "I wish I could get Win to get some modern suits," Aunt Elizabeth continued. "He's so old-fashioned." I had always wanted to take a beau to Aunt Elizabeth's and I passed the evening in possessive bliss as she discussed the trouble with youth in this day and age, and how Uncle Win, when he'd been a man of twenty-two and needed a hobby, had simply gone right out and bought up four hundred acres of orchards and prize cows for something to do. Aunt Elizabeth believed the problem in the world today was that people weren't active enough, didn't we agree?

"Take the colored people," said Aunt Elizabeth as she placed her untouched finger bowl to her left. "My colored girls don't go around expecting to be president or singing in buses through the streets. No, they're busy in the kitchen, that's where they are. They don't have time to be making signs all day long, they've too much to do. If all the colored people had enough to do there wouldn't be any of this nonsense. They should be more active, the colored people. I've been active all my life and have never once thought of protesting a thing. Look at Africa. You don't see civil rights in Africa. That's because they're all busy drumming and dancing about in Africa and haven't the time to be marching down the streets being rude."

After dinner Richard and I thanked Aunt Elizabeth for the lovely evening.

"I hope," Aunt Elizabeth said, touching a finger to Richard's long hair as we were standing at the door, "I do hope you're not like all those other young people in blankets I see on the Esplanade, always doing those unpleasant things to each other all the time. It doesn't seem like much fun. Young people today never seem to have much fun."

October passed in a haze and in November Richard and I got ten dollars per diem to be extras in *Love Story*. For twelve hours a day we sat in the cold stands in the Harvard hockey rink, cheering with different scarves around our necks to represent the different colleges. I was too embarrassed to cheer—I'd never cheered at anything in my life—but I would stand demurely next to Richard in my copper-colored maxi coat while he shouted and gesticulated with an intense gusto. It was kind of exciting for the first day, but we quit by the third because Richard wanted to get back to classes, and my shingles, which I'd gotten in October, were acting up.

"Shingles are a disease of the nervous system, and there's absolutely nothing we can do about them!" the nurse at Stillman Infirmary had said brightly, as if this prognosis was somehow reassuring. For a month I had a wide band of hideous rash bubbling around my waist, forcing me to abandon my tight little skirts for baggy shifts and jeans, and making me so ashamed of my body I wore a bathing suit in the shower. But the worst part was the shooting pains that came without any warning. Richard was as attracted to me as ever, I have to give him that, but to tell you the truth, I never thought he believed me about those pains.

"Place your mind above it," he would say with just a tiny bit of irritation as I stood writhing in the corner of the freezing hockey rink. "Conquer!"

I spent the Wednesday before Thanksgiving over at Boston Rehab, throwing a football with William and Spencer around a tiny dirt courtyard, while Harry watched, a big, lifeless lug.

"Hey, hey, over here!" Spencer yelled, or whatever it is you're supposed to yell when you're having fun tossing around the old football. I wasn't such a great catcher, or thrower for that matter, and my hands were cold, so after a while I went over and stood with Harry against the brick wall, next to a tree that would have been a weed anywhere else, and talked about how great it was going to be when he got out, an occurrence that didn't exactly seem to be right around the corner. About the most optimistic thing Harry had going for him at the time was that the day he had managed to get to the hospital door in the hopes of flinging himself in front of the North Avenue-Broadway, he'd found himself turning back extra slowly to get his coat, because he'd wanted the nurses to catch him. After almost three months in the hospital Harry was still as drugged up as could be and moved like a snail and, although he made perfect sense, spoke only haltingly, and in his eyes was a dull, hopeless look, but I think he believed what I said, just a little, for a second or two, anyway.

After a couple of hours, we kissed him good-bye, and, leaving him there in the day room with the paper turkey on the wall, Spencer and I walked away, turning around once to see Harry, settled in his chair, lift his head with a great effort to stare at the clock to see how many more hours he had until his eight o'clock anxiety attack. Harry had explained to me the day before that an anxiety attack was when you felt suddenly trapped and dying, except it wasn't a physical pain, more like somebody told you they had just opened all the gas jets in the room and locked all the doors and windows. Then we walked quickly out of the hospital so Harry wouldn't see our faces, and drove off in Spencer's car to spend the long weekend with the parents in Westchester County.

It wasn't the most wonderful Thanksgiving in the world, what with Harry in the hospital (Harry told me later that he had cried to see that the cafeteria women in their dead-end jobs had made the effort to wear miniature Pilgrim hats on top of their blue hair) and George's wife being rude to him in front of the rest of the family.

"Here, George, carry these bags" was Dorothy's greeting to the group. "What did I marry you for, anyway?"

111

"Is that why you married my son?" my mother had asked with uncharacteristic sharpness, and the weekend was off to its start.

But none of the bickering affected me as I coasted through the long weekend thinking nonstop about Richard Townsend and knitting these awful scarves that had holes in them every foot or two when I'd had too much wine. Knitting was very big at Harvard that year and in almost every lecture hall you would see great, burly guys with beards working their needles intently. "Gentlemen, please!" one professor had burst out when the clicking got to him. Everyone was to receive a scarf from me that Christmas, except for my father, who kept happening to mention that he never wore scarves, with Richard Townsend getting, as an early gift, the one, the only one, that had been *purled* as well as *knit,* with the result that it curled in at both sides into one long snake. He had sailed around Harvard in it, a long, pea-green rope picking up slush as it ventured farther and farther past his knees.

Spencer drove me back Sunday night, even though he had to be back in New York the following day to take a plane to Mexico, where he was getting an abortion for this girl who, we found out months later, wasn't pregnant, just so desperate to hold on to Spencer, whom she'd slept with on and off for a week in September, she was to go through with the whole charade. Whether he was shielding me or too racked with guilt, Spencer didn't tell me about the abortion that night, just glumly that he was going to Mexico for a two-day vacation and then I kidded him because he couldn't remember the name of the girl he was going with.

Spencer dropped me off at Daniels around nine, and I ran into the dorm to find I had two phone messages from Richard. I rushed up to my room to call, but before I could pick up the phone it rang, and the girl at the desk told me Richard was downstairs. I jumped in the elevator, which was still there, and when the doors opened there was Richard, in a torn

sweater, mussed and out of breath from his leap down to
Radcliffe.

"I love you," he said, and I got a prickly feeling all over
my skin, and in the air I saw sparkles.

Chapter Nine

Probably, though, it was the speed. I'd been eating like a horse since I'd met Richard Townsend, and so, with a daughter's timing, only a daughter could land upon, I'd chosen Thanksgiving to begin my starvation diet, and into my suitcase had gone the vial of yellow and blue pills, which I'd gulped down in pairs in the parents' powder room. The speed made me a little shaky, and I'd already decided I wasn't going to take any more, but that Monday after Thanksgiving I walked into Nat. Sci. 107, and found, to my surprise, the proctors handing out blue books. I had not been to a single class since I'd laid eyes on Richard Townsend, and, to be honest, I did not even know what Nat. Sci. 107 was supposed to be about, although I strongly suspected it had to do with the evolution of man, for there, neatly typed at the top of the exam book was: "Trace the evolution of man." I might have panicked, as I am not gifted at science. Instead, with a bold stroke, I began writing: "The evolution of primate to man was indeed a miraculous one . . . ," which evidently really gave me away because, it turns out, man *is* a primate, though for what purpose I still do not know. "Lucky for early man he had a thumb, enabling him to fashion weapons, making him far, far superior to the animals around him," I continued insightfully, drawing heavily on knowledge I had acquired in elementary school. And then desperately, yet not without insight, I queried: "Or, might we not ask, is this ability to kill a true *superiority?*" And so I was set for the rest of the exam. In 1969 all you had to do was mention war or women's rights and they couldn't touch you with a ten-foot pole.

After this experience I decided I might consider checking in on my other classes to see what was up, with the result I found I had a couple of papers due. Back in my room, I leafed through a book or two from the enormous row of spanking new paperbacks lined up on my desk—they always assigned an impossible number of books to read for each course, as if they never expected you to read anything but the introductions —but all I could think about was Richard Townsend in his dungarees and rumpled flannel shirts. So I took a few more pills and prayed for the inspiration to finish a sentence.

In those days I smoked cigarette after cigarette as if it were a duty (though never in front of Richard Townsend, who was interested in some new thing called ecology and didn't even approve of me shaving my legs), and drank a dozen Tabs a day, and never once did the merest thought about my health flicker across my brian. *Health* was then something of a pejorative word and not one anyone used much except to say "How healthy you look!" meaning, of course, "How fat!" but the speed scared me. The first few days of popping the pills were great—certainly it was the first and last time I was ever to understand symbolism, and how brilliantly I discussed *Desire Under the Elms* and how the elms represented mother's milk, an interpretation so profound that now, as I reread the play, I don't know where in Sam Hill I found any of it—but by the fourth day or so I got wobbly and paranoid and tired, even though my heart was racing. By the end of that week, my papers done—emphatic, enthusiastic, incoherent works with much underlining—I hid the speed again and, suddenly sluggish, dragged myself through the long hours when I wasn't with Richard Townsend.

Richard had told me he loved me the Sunday after Thanksgiving, and he told me again and again on Monday and Tuesday and Wednesday, but by Thursday he was noticeably silent on the subject, and by Saturday morning he confided that he wasn't sure, he'd have to think about it. Richard had a small part in *A Doll's House,* and that Saturday night there was a cast party to which he had wanted to go alone. He was late in returning and I remember feeling pretty stupid waiting for him in his room, or rather his tent, bobbing my head up and down under the sheeted roof now and then, pretending to tidy up or something to let his roommates know I was there, so they wouldn't say anything against me. Finally, around two, Richard arrived home. He had that intense, caring look on his face that I was to learn meant he was about to tell me he didn't care. His eyes bored into mine.

"Winifred Lowe was there tonight," Richard said, with earth-shattering significance. "When I left the party, she took my arm and held it for a moment, looking at me." I think Richard sighed then, lovely in his perplexity, and added thoughtfully, in case I was having trouble picturing it, that Winifred had been wearing a flowing satin shirt. Winifred Lowe was a senior who was playing Nora, and I don't imagine the comparison of Winifred, skinny and other-worldly in her satin shirt, and me, round and cozy as a red apple in my men's sweater from the Coop, did a great deal for my relationship with Richard Townsend. It is hard to believe now that he told me all the details, but somehow I know not only what Winifred was wearing but that her eyes shone, and that night as we lay in bed I cried like a baby in Richard's arms. I knew I was losing him, that it was only a matter of time, that one day I would be all alone, stumbling in the dark.

Two weeks later William, Spencer, Pony, and I trooped up to Boston Rehab for a Christmas Hootenanny the day room

117

was sponsoring, the focal point of which was to be Spencer and Harry playing carols. Spencer hadn't brought his guitar; since the trip to Mexico he had sworn off playing to drive a cab six days a week and eat only brown rice (cooking it up at breakfast, popping it in a jar for lunch, coming home to a pot of it at night) until he could pay back William, even though William said not to worry, the money had been charged off his Diner's Club card, whose bill he never dreamed of paying more than the monthly minimum, and while William didn't know whose money had paid for the abortion, it assuredly hadn't been his. In any case, the theory had been that Spencer would just pick out songs on the piano, but the hospital piano, we saw when we arrived, was all bashed and battered, as if some patient had gotten to it before the Thorazine had gotten to him, and when Spencer, regrouping, tried to sing "Silent Night," with Harry haltingly accompanying him on flute and the rest of the patients staring off into space, Spencer made it only to the fifth bar before breaking into tears. Putting down his flute, Harry walked over to the other end of the day room, returning a few minutes later with a large picture of a star he had evidently just crayoned.

"See, Spencer," Harry said slowly to our brother's broken figure, "I finally made you a star."

That Wednesday, I went home for Christmas vacation, lugging along an enormous suitcase full of books, whose latch my hand was not to graze the entire three weeks. Spencer couldn't be persuaded to give himself even a day off from cab-driving and rice-eating, so I had to take the train, which screeched to a stop at every gray, snowless city between Boston and Stamford, Connecticut. For five hours I stared out a window so dirty it was almost opaque, never glancing around or going to the bathroom lest I'd have to rouse myself and say something chatty like "Excuse me" to the person beside me; I wouldn't even pick up a magazine because exams were held right after Christmas and I felt too guilty to read anything unless it was directly related to a course. My father met me at the station,

118

kissing me and telling me how beautiful I looked, which I think he probably believed, and whistling as he picked up my bags and brought them to the car.

"Really, your mother and I like living here very much," he said more than once during the drive home, but when we arrived at the house you got the impression there wasn't a whole lot of neighbors dropping by for eggnog, what with the *New Yorkers* rigidly lined up on the coffee table next to the neat pile of *Concord Journals* to go through. The parents had always owned old houses, but the one in Bedford Hills was modern and convenient—every piece of soap in the place had a metal disk in the middle (that the parents magically inserted) so it could stick magnetically to the sides of the tubs and sinks, and to open the pine cabinet doors, you had to give them a whack and then you wished to God you'd never opened them as they bounced back at you for about an hour while you tried to get them shut. Most of the lights hadn't been turned on yet and the house seemed empty and cold, even the refrigerator door lacking the usual cheery Art Buchwald–Erma Bombeck type of clippings about the Generation Gap that my mother could never resist putting up, even when she knew such display ended all chance of our ever reading them.

George was off at Dorothy's parents' for what he called, to my father's dismay, "the holidays," so it was just the parents and me sitting around the tree Christmas morning opening Harry's present of one of those yarn pot holders you weave on a little grille. There was some combined theory about holiday traffic and dentist appointments that couldn't be changed to explain why we weren't up visiting Harry, who spent Christmas in the day room opening his gift from the nurses of soap on a rope. For the next two weeks I was miserable and took it out on the parents, refusing to go to *Fiddler on the Roof* with them, even though the tickets had been hard to get, refusing to eat dinner with them every night on the spurious grounds it was making me fat, refusing even to come down the stairs to say hello to their friends the Hamblyns, for fear I might

119

have to stir myself into a smile. Finally, to the considerable relief of all, I went back to Cambridge, desperate to see Richard and willing to do anything for him.

Richard had moved during the break, and was now living with Gil, a tall sophomore who was always giving you a penetrating glance. He'd managed to get his own bedroom, which would have been great, except that when I called him the second I got back, he said he just wanted to be very good friends, meaning, of course, that he never wanted to lay eyes on me again as long as he lived.

"I need to be free, Elizabeth," Richard said, and so it was only once or twice a week throughout the winter that I knocked at A-12, dropped my maxi coat in a heap on the living-room floor, and went with Richard into his room, where, though just good friends, we found ourselves on the bed in the space of a minute. The sex was even better than before, probably because nobody was supposed to know about it, in that I wasn't officially Richard's girlfriend, and now more than ever would I gladly have given up my virginity to Richard as a doormat upon which to wipe his feet. But no, said Richard as he crammed me half-dressed into a closet one afternoon at the sound of Gil's key in the door, it was not right.

When Gil and Richard decided to throw a party in their rooms—I think it was in honor of the Ides of March, or some such pretentious holiday—I was invited, though, of course, it was made clear to me, not as Richard's date. When I arrived, the suite was crowded with a bunch of people I didn't know, or know well, including Sophie Riolo, who threw me a caring, sympathetic look, which I needed like a hole in the head, and everyone was very cool, wearing jeans and sitting cross-legged around the fire. They were mostly from the Loeb crowd and so were very relaxed, what with their back-rub history uniting them. I always wore baggy jeans and sloppy sweaters, but I had chosen that night to don a royal-blue rayon shift, which was supposed to make me look thinner, but in which I resem-

120

bled an overweight secretary, and even the pantyhose I'd bought had turned out to be thick support hose. When they passed around the pot I took some, even though I hadn't smoked any since high school, but instead of feeling light and silly I got suddenly depressed. I withdrew into a corner of the pea-green corduroy couch that every guy in the world always has, and watched Richard talking to Sophie Riolo for a while, and then I went into his room and shut the door.

I sat glued to Richard's bed, staring at his alarm clock for two straight hours as it ground inexorably forward. It was one of those new digital models in which a little white card flipped over with a churn and a click to keep you posted as to the precise moment that each minute passed, which I suppose would have been invaluable for someone with a schedule a bit more packed than mine. At 11:54 people started leaving, and by 12:34 everybody had gone except for Richard and Wendy Marx, who was an old high school friend of Gil's. I had heard a lot about Wendy and how smart and interesting she was, because Gil had always had a crush on her, of which nothing had ever come. It was not, perhaps, a pastime I would have chosen, listening to Richard and Wendy really getting to know each other—I had a ringside seat, since they were sitting against the wall that abutted Richard's room—but they soon began to talk in the quiet, intense tones that always meant you were about to kiss. I stuck to the bed, paralyzed for seventeen minutes, all of us waiting for the kiss, which I was to be spared, I realized, when at 12:58 they left to take a walk along the Charles. After a few minutes I dragged myself from the room and rode my bike through the slush back to Radcliffe, the torn lining of my maxi coat catching in the spokes.

I didn't wake up the next morning till noon. It was Sunday and gray and raw, as only Sundays know how to be, and the chapel bells clanging a modern, discordant tune didn't exactly make it any cozier. I felt empty all right, but for some reason wasn't in the mood for crying. Probably my body had just

121

dried up from all the crying I'd filled up my calendar with since coming back from Christmas vacation. I pulled on some clothes and went down to the dining hall, where I ate a couple of wads of some indecipherable stuff covered in gravy, then returned to my room, stretching out on my bed like a beached whale. The only good thing about being really full up with dorm food was that you felt too sick to think about anything. Then the phone rang.

"Gil is here to see you," announced the girl at the desk.

When I saw Gil's face I didn't have to be Jeanne Dixon to guess he wasn't there to deliver some really great news.

"Elizabeth," he said, with a long face, as if this said it all, and I took him past Alison, who was sitting on her bed facing the wall, around the corner to my section. Our room was L-shaped, with my little settlement in the foot, which allowed Alison and me to lead separate lives of despair. Alison had broken up with the heavy beau over Christmas and had settled onto her bed to face the wall day after day for two months, wrapped in a blanket like an Indian squaw.

"Richard asked me to come," Gil said, dropping into the chair by the desk. "It's Richard and Wendy, Liz. Last night they met and were drawn together like this," and he demonstrated for me by bringing his hands together and clasping them tightly. "Richard says it's hard to know where it will lead, but it's leading somewhere. It's one of those things that happens once in a lifetime, there's no stopping it," Gil continued, not without drama, and for a moment I wondered why I was the one getting all the pity when Gil was supposedly so in love with this Wendy, and then he was good enough to fill in the gaps on her character. "I've know her since high school, Elizabeth," he assured me—you would have thought I was Richard's mother, for God's sake. "She's a wonderful person."

For the next month I caught up on my sleep, you might say, sometimes slumbering eighteen hours a day, dreaming wonderful dreams of Richard saying actually he was kidding, he still loved me. The dreams were so ordinary and so real, you couldn't blame me for plunging back to sleep whenever I woke up. "I wish I were dead, I wish I were dead," I would comfort myself over and over when the laws of nature required me to stay awake for an hour or two, sometimes switching over to a couple of halfhearted I'm going to go crazy's, until finally I found myself yawning again.

"I just can't believe that you haven't always been perfectly happy," my father said to me years later, when, as if it were some kind of graduation, the parents proudly came to the last of my shrink sessions under their financial auspices, and in a way I almost know what he was trying to say. I mean, I was only nineteen, at Harvard, with the world ahead of me, and yet it was this time that was the worst time in my life, because I had lost the essential, moronic belief of my family that everything always worked out happily in the end, the belief that had enabled generations to sweep in and out of insane asylums on the way to the symphony to chat with one deranged relative or another. It was gone—I suppose it had started to go when my other great belief, Harry, had toppled eight years before, and I didn't know what to do but lie huddled in my bed day after day, listening for the gentle, random clickings of the control box of my electric blanket and waiting for the hours to pass me by.

I left my room only to go visit Harry or pick up a six-pack or two of ice cream sandwiches. Through the black snow I would trudge to the deli on Mass. Ave., where I'd make up stories for the merchant, who didn't speak English, to explain why I needed so many ice cream sandwiches and Twinkies and bagels. "Par-ty!" I would shout, as if it were only volume that impeded our communication, and, whenever I had the energy, I would act out the festivities with a pathetic charade. Then back I would trudge and gulp down the ice cream sandwiches quickly before they melted, finally, mercifully drifting back to sleep, waking again in the night for feedings like a baby.

It got to be that the bright part of my day was in the afternoon, when, as I had since the early, brilliant days of fall,

I took the cruddy North Avenue-Broadway local over to the outskirts of Boston to visit Harry. I would sit with him in the pulsing heat of the day room, under the Have a Nice Day sign, and talk and talk about Richard Townsend while Harry listened. Harry still didn't say much, it was too hard, and then, there wasn't usually a whole lot of news. Everyone chain-smoked there—not like friends but slowly and deliberately, immobilized by the Thorazine—and I was Queen of the May because I had matches and could light everyone's cigarettes. At three the nurse came in with the medication, and it was almost like a party, with her passing around a tray of little paper cups.

Nothing much had changed with Harry over the past few months, except now, instead of weaving pot holders, he was painting giant, wild watercolors. They must have taken him forever to complete, because his movements were still painfully slow, but crazy mess after mess he came forth with until one day out of the blue he painted a picture of a stick-figure boy playing his saxophone for a yellow-haired girl sitting in the window of a little house. The great thing about the picture was that it looked exactly as if a seven-year-old had done it, with a green line at the bottom for the ground and a blue line at the top and in the corner a wedge of sun, one yellow ray carefully surrounded by blue so as not to turn the sky green.

"Here, this is for you," Harry said, handing me the picture. "It's me playing my saxophone to you there in the house," he continued in his deliberate way, and on the sun he wrote: "To Lizzie from Harry."

After visiting Harry, I would return to clear off a resting place in the heap of trash, magazines, and clothes that made up my room, and continue my dozing, half on my bed and half on the floor. We all put our mattresses on the floor in those days—it was the first thing you did when you moved into a new room—and late one evening when the phone rang, I rolled over and my cheek landed on a sticky ice cream sandwich wrapper; for a split second I thought I had woken up in

124

the wastebasket. I picked up the phone and tried to make it sound as if I hadn't been asleep, clearing my throat.

"Excuse me," I said, instead of hello, but it didn't matter because it turned out to be Harry. "Harry?" I asked, surprised because I'd never known him to call anyone from Boston Rehab.

"Guess what," said Harry in a voice that almost had some life, "I just read a whole book."

"You what?"

"I read a whole book," repeated Harry, who hadn't been able to read a single sentence since October, or wash his hair or shave or even turn himself over in bed, and then his voice became a little whisper. "I've been throwing away my Thorazine. Don't tell anyone. Every day I pretend to take it and then I throw it away. They're letting me out next week for a whole day."

There was an eclipse that year, and it was on that day Harry came out, not that I paid eclipses any truck. When we were kids and there was an eclipse, it was really special because there was an eclipse only every one hundred years, and Harry had drawn up all these complicated charts none of us understood and gotten everybody up at dawn and over to Nashawtuc Hill, where half of Concord was standing around with dark glasses so they wouldn't go blind, but then the next thing you knew they were having eclipses every other day. Harry and I had planned to go see Genet's *The Blacks,* which a big theater company was performing over at the Loeb, but when we got to the theater we decided we couldn't stand seeing something meaningful, and turned away. Just as we were leaving, I spotted Richard Townsend. Richard had met Harry once when he'd come along to Boston Rehab. The visit had not been a success, with Richard a touch uncomfortable sitting next to the girl with the pacifier, but he pretended to be glad to run into us.

"It's good to see you again, Harry," he said in a booming voice, extending his hand and looking very puny.

"So," said Harry in his slow way, "how are you treating my sister these days?" Richard winced, and you might have felt sorry for him if you had it in you.

"Not so good, I guess," he said flatly.

"Scum," said Harry. It was barely discernible but Richard heard it and I heard it, and then I laughed and Harry laughed and we walked away, leaving Richard just standing there.

Harry and I walked over to Harvard Yard, and then everything got dark and eerie for a moment on account of the eclipse and then the sun came out. Through the open dorm windows came the Beatles singing "Here Comes the Sun," and Harry and I walked together through the gates out to the Square.

It was pretty mild the day that Harry and I spent wandering around Harvard Square. I know it was warm because I was wearing this awful pink paisley tent dress—when you're overweight you always wear clothes you would never wear in a million years if you were thin—and I looked like some fat girl whose grandmother had taken her shopping. I billowed along like a beach ball in the April breezes beside Harry, a giant specter, but I didn't care; I was so happy to be with Harry, walking outside.

Chapter Ten

Harry got better every day. He was talking almost normally now and reading books, and he even wrote a poem. It was called "The First Day of Spring It Snowed," not a very cheery title, but what do you expect. His shrink at Boston Rehab wouldn't let him leave, though, until he told her why he was getting better. Her theory was that he was falling in love with her and why didn't he come out and admit it? Harry's theory was that he didn't want to hurt her feelings, but she was the ugliest woman he'd ever met, although this was a sentiment he did not share with her. Not that he shared much of anything with her, certainly not the whole story, which even I didn't know at the time, which was that Harry had been saving up the Thorazine pills in the first place in order to kill himself, and then to his surprise he had started feeling better. Nor could he tell her simply that he'd been throwing away the Thorazine for fear they'd start stuffing it down his throat, so he kept coming up with different reasons for his improvement. No good, his shrink would say, eyes wet with sympathy as she imagined Harry struggling against his love. So in May, Harry was still in the hospital.

But he was coming out for whole days fairly often and we were hanging around together and, after a dark winter burrowed in my bed with ice cream sandwiches, things were looking up. The parents came several times to visit Harry and one Sunday we all went over to Spencer's to sit on cushions on the floor and eat a macrobiotic dinner of seaweed soup that looked like spiders in water and whole-wheat apple pie that, if you could believe it, had no sugar in it. Still, it was an improvement on the all-rice diet that had turned Spencer's face green, and on which he had subsisted until early March, when he'd gone up to Maine to assist in a film on the maharishi. The moment he'd arrived, Spencer said, he had happened to look through a window and see the maharishi gesturing upward with his arm, like a song, and Spencer's knees, in his cadaver state, had simply buckled under him in relief, bringing him to the ground as he realized that life wasn't supposed to be hard, that he'd been going about it the exact opposite way from the teaching he'd been trying to follow, that all of it should be taken as easily as the wave of the maharishi's arm.

Spencer and Pony were living in an apartment off Harvard Square with a beautiful, wraithlike girl named Anna who had brick-red hair and huge circles under her eyes and looked the way people in movies who are supposed to be drug addicts look. She wore ragged peasant blouses and carpenter pants and was very somber. It was hard to tell whom she was having an affair with on a given day—eventually I think she worked her way through everyone in Spencer's circle, including Harry, on a half-day leave from the loony bin. Harry told me later that he spent an entire two-hour group therapy session back at Boston Rehab explaining Anna's generosity to the group and the jealousy it had evoked, drawing triangles and various other geometric shapes on the chalkboard, while everyone sat riveted, including the intern from Harvard Medical School who had just been assigned to the hospital to begin his training. Anyway, Anna was always involved with someone who was

128

about (it turning out, of course, that she hated men—she eventually moved to an island in Greece), because whenever you arrived at Spencer's apartment, the air would be heavy with meaning.

She was there that day and so was Pony, who said hello to me in a low voice, and it was quite a scene with them and Harry and Mother, in a snappy gray pantsuit, and my father chatting away with Anna about heaven knows what, though I must say it was the first time I ever heard Anna laugh. The original plan had been to go to Loch Obers, but Spencer had insisted upon cooking the dinner, and he'd spent the whole day preparing for us, wracked with decisions like whether to splurge on granola even though he was a strict macrobiotic and could not eat honey, and we all said how good it was, even poor Harry, for whom getting a good meal was about it when it came to looking forward to things.

After dinner, Spencer burned incense and served us bowls of herbal tea that tasted like perfume, while all of us, except the parents, puffed away on strong cigarettes, clashing with the sickly sweetened air. At one end of the table Anna explained to my father about the cubes she sold when she wasn't being a telephone operator, while my mother listened brightly to something Pony had jumped up and brought back to read; at the other end, I talked with Harry, who smoked a big cigar from the drugstore, while Spencer sat with one knee up, balancing a Camel in his mouth as he picked out on the guitar a song he was writing about an Indian warrior, which, early in creation, consisted of the same phrase over and over.

Spencer had a kind of holy promiscuity now; instead of just loving him, the girls worshiped him. He got them all to meditate and they all said how they were really glad to have known him even after he dropped them in a few days. Harry told me that afternoon how it almost killed him when Spencer had walked into Boston Rehab that week with Leslie, the girl Harry had finally gotten back to his apartment two years before and then gotten too depressed to do anything about it.

129

Leslie and Spencer, whom she'd met only once at a bar when Harry'd been playing, had just run into each other in Harvard Square, but Harry had been able to tell something was going to happen between them by the glow on Leslie's face. Two years earlier, Harry had spent a whole day driving his motorcycle up and down the streets of Brighton, where he thought Leslie had said she lived, though he wasn't sure, just to apologize for getting so depressed that night. "I still would gladly give my life for her, such as it is," Harry said to me, "even though I know down deep she's just a nothing," but it had been Spencer who had given her a pat on the head three days later, and sent her on her way.

We were an odd lot, all right, that Sunday at Spencer's, sitting around that table that had once been a door, but we had a nice time, if you compared it to the times we were used to having.

I'd been taking the diet pills off and on again that April, as a transition from lying in bed all day to getting up now and then, and by the beginning of May, with things going better, I flushed what I had left down the toilet—at least most of them; I couldn't bear to flush them all. I needed about two weeks of dragging myself around to get over the withdrawal, holding onto parking meters for dear life like an old drunk as I journeyed from Radcliffe to Harvard Square. Sometimes it took me an entire day to charge a bottle of conditioner, and back I would huff to my room, clutching my accomplishment to my bosom. Finally I found I wasn't shaking in the mornings, and I figured it was time to get back into the swing of living. The best way, I decided, was to go about mechanically doing things as if I cared until one day, magically, I *would* care. This was a theory I had picked up in Sunday school, where they told you to pray a lot, all the time and for anything you wished, and the next thing you knew you would start believing. It hadn't seemed fair that you could pray for something as selfish as a bicycle ("That's okay, too!" promised the teachers), so I had saved up my prayers for Spencer, who had accidentally let the Andrews' dog Pal out the back door ("Who let Pal out that morning?" the Andrews still ask) and he had been run over by a school bus, which of course severely tried my religious beliefs. Still, the concept of be mechanical and then you will believe somehow stuck with me and I set about finding things to keep me going.

It never occurred to me to occupy myself by going to classes, so I went over to the Loeb to sign up to work on *Julius Caesar*, for which they were already in rehearsal. I met with, or rather threw myself at the feet of, the stage manager, a brusque, short-haired girl who said, as if she were sweeping crumbs from the table, that, all right, I could be assistant stage manager. This meant I was vaguely in charge of props, which they didn't actually need, because it was a minimalist production, with the set consisting of blocks of wood strewn about and everybody miming picking up glasses of water, or swords or helmets, or whatever the theatrical business required. Mainly what I did was to go to rehearsals and sit around wearing jeans and bright men's shirts I'd charged at the Coop.

I was low man on the totem pole over at the Loeb. The tall, bony girls who had long, straight hair and parts in the play would breeze past me as if I didn't exist, but I was still too weak from the speed withdrawal to care. I would putter about in my pink shirt, trying to look as if I were doing something, happy simply to be there and not lying on my mattress on the floor staring up at the ceiling. Then one day I noticed this freshman. I knew he was a freshman because he was one of The Rabble and the only line he got to say, naked to the waist, was "Peace, ho!" and even that was in unison. Probably he was tired of doing all those growling like cats and dogs exercises every night to get in character, but at any rate, he generally had a smirk on his face, which tended to make him stand out. At the Loeb everyone was open and honest and looked at you with feeling warmth.

Tommy McGuire was from Ohio and he was really screwed up about being torn between the Midwest and Harvard. I've gone out with a lot of guys from the Midwest and I am never quite sure what it is about their background that leaves them so confused, but I think it's that everyone in the Midwest is a regular guy. They like me because I look like a regular girl with my red cheeks and straight-from-the-hayfields smile, which gives them their Midwest, and then of course on the inside I'm all neurotic, which gives them their East Coast. Anyway, Tommy's face lit up when I walked over to him, and for some reason the first thing out of my mouth was "Can you tell me which one of those guys over there is Gus Horton?"

Gus Horton was someone I'd had a crush on all my life. He was from a big family in Virginia and his grandmother had been a neighbor of my grandmother, which means they lived only half a mile apart, and they would get together in the evenings to play checkers and drink gin. Gus was always very cool, making jokes in that prep school way as he shot billiards in his grandmother's game room, and I don't remember ever having the nerve to speak to him until we were fourteen and his parents stopped by our house in Concord. They were taking Gus up to Choate, and I remember him sitting in the chintz wing chair in our living room, tall and yellow-haired and very assured, as I came down the stairs. "Oh hi," I said in an offhand manner without stopping, and bounded out the front door. Story after story had filtered back of all Gus's accomplishments at Choate, acting awards, tennis trophies, early acceptance at Harvard, but always he had been in the distance, a superior creature. Then that September, before signing up for *People vs. Leech,* I had tried out for the freshman acting seminar, which was nearly impossible to get into. I hadn't auditioned well in years, so I'd popped a few diet pills and a package of Energets for breakfast, and coming down from them that afternoon had given a rather affecting reading as a weepy Juliet. I had actually cried and shaken, and even though the scene was supposed to be a joyous one, I could tell the professor had been impressed. My heart had pounded the next day as I scurried off to the Loeb to find the list of acceptances, and when I finally forced myself to look at the sheet, I saw eleven names. The tenth name was Gus Horton's, and beneath, as first alternate, was my own.

It turned out Tommy was good friends with Gus, who was also a member of The Rabble, though he had a name, Citizen 4, and got to say, "Ay, and wisely," all by himself. Gus had a lot of different ways of playing his part and I must say, he was quite good, though not terribly vital to the play. The play pretty much took up our lives, but when we weren't in rehearsal, the three of us would go lie on top of one of the dorms in Harvard Yard and smoke cigarettes. One night, after I went home, they flipped a coin to see who would go out with me, and Tommy won.

It hadn't occurred to me to pin my hopes on Gus, anyway —for one thing I wasn't thin enough yet—so Tommy and I started to spend out spare time sitting on my bed in Daniels, necking and talking about how depressed we were. One bright spring afternoon, Tommy said he wanted to meet Harry, and we hitched over to Boston Rehab, where for three hours he and Harry talked against phony intellectuals at Harvard, and I couldn't get a word in edgewise. As we were leaving, Harry whispered to me that Tommy reminded him of himself, meaning it as a great compliment. My heart was still with Richard, but I liked Tommy, even though he lacked the drippy sentimentality that is so helpful to sex when you're young.

The student strike hit us on a lovely evening in early May. *Julius Caesar* was in dress rehearsal and I was sitting on the linoleum floor of the green room talking to Tommy McGuire when in rushes this kid in a loincloth, shouting either "They bombed Cambodia!" or "They shot some students at Kent State!" I'm not sure which came first, horrible as it sounds. I was a bit hazy on the actual facts behind the strike even then. This is because I'd stopped reading the newspaper in the eighth grade, a bad call that has put me on thin ice ever since, considering the times in which I have lived. Now I think of it, I realize it was Kent State, because I remember that I was at that moment clutching a pamphlet titled "The History of Vietnam," which I'd been carrying with me everywhere that spring, always, as Tommy noticed, on page seven—and the next thing you knew everyone was running around, half-dressed in sheets and cardboard, saying, "Oh my god, oh my god."

"We've got to do something!" cried Mark Antony, and there was all kinds of hubbub and then someone produced red arm bands, which everyone put on, except for Tommy Mc-Guire, who pulled me aside and said, "Let's get out of here and go back to your room." By now the cast and crew were rushing out of the Loeb, and moving in a mass down Brattle Street. "But everyone's going to the rally in the Yard!" I said longingly, my red arm band burning importantly on my arm.

Tommy stood there looking at me. "All right, Liz," he said and we walked over to the Yard, where everyone was marching around in a circle holding placards and chanting away about capitalist pigs. My heart beat quickly, my life finally taking on purpose.

"I don't know," said Tommy, standing away from the crowd, "it's pretty confusing."

"What do you mean you don't *know?* We're on *strike,* Tommy, we've just *got* to stop the bombing in Cambodia," I said hotly, hoping I'd gotten the country right and secretly vowing to finish my Vietnam pamphlet, which I held still against my chest.

Unfortunately, I was never to have the time. The next morning I had to go to three meetings at Radcliffe, strident meetings with the type of girls who always sit in the front row in class and know every answer, triumphantly presiding. Lucky for me, it didn't matter that I didn't even know where Vietnam *was* because mostly all anyone talked about was parliamentary procedure. "Point of order!" I called out from time to time just to keep in the thick of things.

Much more interesting was the big assembly that afternoon of the cast and crew of *Julius Caesar*. We all filed into the auditorium with solemn faces, and then all the actors and actresses made impassioned speeches that didn't make much sense but sure sounded great.

"It's exactly like *this!*" said the incredibly good-looking guy who played Octavius, gesturing with both arms toward the ceiling, and everyone cheered. After much debate, with everyone steamily on the same side, it was decided that it would be wrong to continue performing *Julius Caesar,* the reasoning being a trifle unclear to me even then, and with a nod of my head I agreed to give up my job as prop girl, if that's what it took to stop the escalation in Vietnam. What I remember best is swaying at the top of the auditorium, my arms around Gus Horton and a dozen people in a group hug, crying in fervor, while Tommy McGuire stood down on the edge of the stage, dry-eyed and shaking his head. Then the professor in charge of the production, who hadn't said anything up till then, called for quiet and made the final speech.

"I think you're all making a mistake," he said. "In a couple of weeks, this will all feel like bad sex."

The Strike of 1970 meant you refused to go to classes—I was a bit ahead of my time, in that I hadn't gone to classes since September—and also that you refused to take exams. I couldn't help feeling a little guilty as I went around to my instructors informing them that I would not be taking my finals, seeing as how it was not exactly what you'd call an enormous sacrifice. It reminded me of how I had given up fish for Lent every year so I wouldn't have to eat it when I went to somebody's house. And since the teaching fellows greeted your announcement with "Right on," you got the feeling you weren't going to flunk out. Of course, most everyone got A's in the end, which was particularly hard on a friend of Tommy's who'd been trying to flunk out all year, in order to prove to his father that he ought to be back on the ranch in Texas herding cattle.

The only professor who wasn't pleased as punch that I was not taking his exam was my Latin teacher. I had taken Latin I to fulfill my language requirement because I thought it would be a gut, in that I had already had three years of Latin in high school, where I'd coasted by on account of a foggy teacher who read the dictionary every night and still regaled his classes about the time Harry Reade had conducted a debate in Latin on why man should walk on all fours.

"But everyone else will be taking the exam, Miss Reade," said the youngish assistant professor, who was dressed in a drab suit from the 1950s and who squinted as if the brightness of my clothes hurt his eyes.

"I must let my conscience be my guide," I said sternly. "Please give me an F on the exam," and I swept out of the office, my arm band fluttering behind me.

It was a busy time, what with your pick of organizations having meetings every two seconds. Then when you got sick of everyone yelling at each other about who had the right to speak next, you got to go out into the streets and stop pedestrians and talk to them about why we shouldn't be fighting in Vietnam, hoping, if you were me, they wouldn't ask you to be too specific. In my spare time I'd go back to my room and write inspired but incoherent and largely illegible thirteen-page letters to the parents, illustrated with all kinds of arrows and indecipherable inserts. What the parents gained from these is doubtful, as they had discovered the war in 1966 and had been liberal at cocktail parties for years. It had been hard in high school to be more politically correct than my mother, who had a personally signed letter from Eugene McCarthy hanging over her desk thanking her for licking envelopes, and so I had gone the other way: "I'm a benevolent monarchist" had been my line. The parents knew a heck of a lot more about Vietnam than I, Miss Johnny-come-lately, but then they always listened to youth, no matter what they had to say, because they honestly believed we were the hope of our country. Considering who their children were, you had to admire them.

Tommy McGuire spent most of the strike sitting around a gas station in Somerville, but what really griped me was when he refused to go to Washington with me.

"I just can't do it, Elizabeth," he said when I cornered him one day on my way to roll in front of some army trucks we'd just heard were in town. "You can't ask me to. I just want to go to Wyoming and join the rodeo."

"I cannot believe that you will not go to Washington and march against the war in Vietnam," I said, "I can*not* believe it!" and off I huffed in search of the military vehicles, which turned out only to be two guys from the National Guard, at whom a bunch of us jeered for a while until, getting no reaction, we turned around and went back to the dorms for dinner.

Among the other people I tried to corral into accompanying me down south was Harry, who said that personally he couldn't drum up much feeling for the march. "In my day, we had panty raids," Harry said, "and if you ask me, they made a lot more sense." He and William had led a panty raid their freshman year, and when Dean Codgeman caught them, victoriously lacy, over at Radcliffe he'd thundered, "I never want to see your faces again." Still, Harry agreed to go down to Washington with me just for the ride, but then he couldn't get the day off from his job. Harry had graduated to getting lithium now at the hospital, along with the Thorazine (it was some trick, he told me, to swallow the lithium and at the same time tongue the Thorazine pill so he could throw it away later when nobody was looking), and they were allowing him to work during the day, as long as he returned to the hospital at night. Harry had applied for a couple of low-level jobs, giving out Spencer's and Pony's number as his home phone, but Pony forgot when the first employer called and gave them the hospital number. "Boston Mental Rehabilitation Center!"

the personnel lady from AT&T had been greeted with when she called, but somehow Harry had managed to explain it all away and get hired as messenger over ten other applicants, to be promoted to decoder the second day, when they found he'd gone to Harvard. Harry said the job was so easy he finished *The Rise and Fall of the Third Reich* the first week.

I remained determined to go down to Washington, even though I had no way to get there except by riding down with my cousin Art in his SDS van. Both William and Art were still active members of SDS, but I wasn't sure if I wanted to go that far, as if the degree of my radicalism would have made the slightest bit of difference to a flea. William had participated in the takeover of University Hall the year before—generally, whenever there was a protest on campus the same picture would crop up in the *Harvard Crimson* with William in the forefront, a nauseated look on his handsome face, raising an arm rather weakly in his beautifully pressed work shirt—but, as he himself readily admitted, it was only by accident and misinformation in the wake of that earlier protest that he had become a leading voice for the movement. It was two days after 400 police officers, including state police, had rushed the occupied hall, arresting 250 and injuring dozens—and William was just one of many at the massive SDS meeting convened in Lowell Lecture Hall to decide what was to be done. William said it had looked like the vote would be against striking, after a member of the accommodating right wing of the party had argued convincingly that student involvement in the government of the university was the true goal, and everyone was nodding agreement when William had been tapped on the shoulder by a prominent left winger of the "storm the winter palace" branch of the organization, who probably knew he would never be called upon to speak and thought to prop William up with some incendiary information. "An article in the *Wall Street Journal* this morning advised the universities that the way to quiet campus protesters was to bust early and then give them student power," he said, and William's hand had shot up in the sea of hands demanding to be called upon. The moderator, possibly too intimidated to refuse a black student the right to speak, had called upon William, who proceeded to repeat the sentence just uttered to him, and instantly the mood of the crowd had swung around from one of accommodating the university to chanting "Strike! Strike!" It was several days until William, after being quoted on the front page by the *Crimson,* realized that not only had he not read the article he'd quoted from, but that no such article had even existed.

In any case, after his burst into the limelight on the eve of the '68 strike, William had become a popular and elegant speaker at all the SDS rallies, making such a splash at one demonstration my year that the law school kicked him out for a semester, honoring him with new status in all of our eyes. I was enrolled that spring in a course, an adjunct of Soc. Sci. 109, which William was teaching until he was suspended, and which consisted of William handing out illegible but wonderful-smelling mimeographed sheets and smudgy xeroxes of Progressive Labor Party newsletters when the class met once a week in his Central Square apartment with the floor that sloped gently downhill from the bathroom to the living room ("You never told me you'd moved to a fun house," Spencer had said the first time he visited). It had been a couple of radicals and me taking the course, and I had biked over a few times, but I could never figure out what anyone was talking about. Mostly it was William asking questions and an unattractive frizzy-haired girl with unshaved legs barking at everyone, as if she held us all responsible for the plight of the working class or something.

William was already in Washington discussing whether they were going to throw rocks or bottles, or whatever they discussed at those interminable meetings, so I decided to take the ride with Art, making it *crystal* clear that I was going to part from the SDS contingent just as soon as we arrived in Washington. It was an all-night drive, with a stop in New

Haven to pick up an SDS printing press, so I threw a couple of diet pills in my mouth and jumped in. When we got to Washington we noticed the Hare Krishna from the Square had made it down before us.

"Oh no," said a guy from the University of Chicago, "those are *our* Hare Krishna." I moved along on the outskirts of the radical groups during the march, and then, when SDS was thinking maybe they'd have to get a little action going, I separated from them and spent the rest of the day kind of canvassing the town by sitting around and bothering people at lunch counters. Miraculously I found Art at the end of the day, and Art, fueled by his cause, and I, by the pills of Dr. Herman Klinck, drove all night back.

Two days later, I broke up with Tommy McGuire. I mean, I didn't say, I can no longer go out with someone who refuses to go down to Washington and harass people as they try to eat their apple pie, but the implication was in the air. Tommy said later he had gotten the picture when he came to my room and found a pack of cigarettes he'd left behind taped to the door with a note saying I was out, and then he heard the water running inside. What had actually happened was that I had downed the last of the diet pills that afternoon and decided to wash my hair and wrap it around my head. Tommy had no idea, of course, that my hair wasn't naturally straight, so I'd taped the cigarettes and note on the door in case he dropped by. Unfortunately, I had just turned the faucet on as I heard him walk up to the door. I couldn't turn it off, because then he'd know someone was inside, so I made the executive decision to leave it running, and stood frozen, my hand on the faucet, waiting for Tommy to make the next move. He knocked twice, tried the door, and then I listened to him walking away. I breathed a sigh of relief, figuring I was out of the woods, but then he came back, with, it became clear, the super. He was worried that the water might be flooding the room, I heard him explain—why suddenly he had to be such a good citizen I do not know—and when the super unlocked the door, there I stood in my bathrobe with hunks of wet hair rounding my head like a turban.

"Oh, excuse me!" the super said, and Tommy didn't even look in. He just turned and walked away.

After a limp June afternoon of handing out anti-war pamphlets in Harvard Square, I got on a bus and returned to the parents' house in Westchester to lie on the floor of my father's den and smoke cigarettes. I was into my third or fourth week of this activity when one afternoon Harry called.

Harry had been dishonorably discharged from the hospital in mid-June, after he finally admitted he'd been crumbling the Thorazine pills down the drain in the water fountain. They were furious at Boston Rehab, and had warned in a hurt tone, don't you ever come back, ever, which, if you asked me, seemed a bit childish for a group of psychiatrists, and Harry said, don't worry, he had no intention of ever returning, fun as it had been. Harry had become so disdainful of shrinks he was seriously considering putting out his own shingle that summer and charging people five bucks an hour to come and rap with him about their problems.

"I know at least as much as those shrinks, and think of the money people would save," Harry pointed out over the phone to me, as I sat defiling the cover of *The First Circle*, which had been sitting by my mother's side of the bed with a little marker in it for two years, and I had to admit he had a point.

Harry was calling from his new apartment in East Cambridge—he'd gotten some government grant he hadn't even applied for, which paid for his living expenses and tuition for Harvard Summer School. "Typical," he said, "no money for anything when you're just some schmuck struggling along, and then you go stark raving mad and the government falls all over itself trying to reward you." Harry had decided to take a double intensive German course that summer because he said he couldn't bear being back at Harvard unless he found some course that wouldn't have any bullshit, but even then he was

141

to have a headache the entire term, just being back at college, though he would receive an A plus in the course.

After hanging up, I wandered back into the den and, feeling a bit livelier than usual, browsed around my father's things, which included a huge collection of swing and Dixieland 78 RPM records, one of which you would frequently be asked to choose so my father could shout out the flip side, and a shelf of books on the Civil War, which, if not exactly pro-Confederate, implied that, while not necessarily as correct as one would have liked on the issues, the losing side had contained the greater proportion of gentlemen. Then there was the filing cabinet the parents had bought years ago to keep track of our achievements. I looked myself up under *"E"* and found one report card from the third grade and a clipping from the *Concord Journal* about the train that fell into the backyard, in which all of us were mentioned. Neatly underlined was "and Lizzie, 10." I was going to check under my brothers' names to see if the same article was there, but it was time for supper.

The original plan had been for me to live with George that summer, over on West 107th Street, while I was attending the Neighborhood Playhouse, a drama school my mother had gone to when it was in its heyday, with Martha Graham teaching dance and Marilyn Monroe coming in for private lessons. Mother was twenty at the time and beautiful and talented, and after she'd graduated she'd been up for a lead on Broadway, but when she'd arrived at the audition and seen her competition, a flashy platinum blonde with hungry eyes, she had gathered her things together without a word and left the office. It was then, she said, that she realized her burning ambition in life was to be a housewife and raise children, probably to compensate for the fact that the only domestic thing her mother ever did was lock up her little girls in the attic closet to cure tantrums. "Say what you will, but I'm my own boss. If I wake up in the morning and decide to look at the fall leaves with Mrs. Andrews instead of doing the laundry, who's to stop me?" my mother used to argue in defense of her choice, when of course the real truth, I learned many years later, was that she'd woken up with a raging headache most mornings, wondering if she would indeed get the bowls of hot oatmeal on the table by seven, and then spent most of the day worrying about whether to serve rice or potatoes for supper—so driven to make everyone happy, she'd wound up, by the fourth baby, in the mental hospital for two years.

Mother and I had decided I should live with George when drama school started in July to help keep him from getting all depressed about the fact that Dorothy, after carefully removing all the lamps from the living room, had rushed off to Reno, as if she couldn't stand being married to George another minute. George was pretty sad, but he didn't want to bother anyone about it. I, however, was good enough to explain to him what I thought love was all about.

"For me, it was a real physical sensation," I said, during my first hour in the apartment, "with chills running up and down my spine."

"Gee, maybe I wasn't ever really in love with Dorothy at all," said George and then felt bad that he'd never been in love.

"I am older now, and so much wiser," I continued later that night when we were watching TV, although I knew down deep that all Richard had to do was to show up and say hi and I'd have been his for all time. George was always great to watch TV with because he knew the name of every actor that had ever been on. "Where have you *been!*" he would say exasperatedly when you had to admit you didn't know whom Bob Newhart had just passed on the street. "That's the guy who played the brother of the milkman on 'December Bride'!"

The second day I lived with George was a Sunday, and I decided to cheer things up for him by greeting him when he returned from singing at church with the cozy smell of Shake 'n Bake chicken, a lovely concept except that I couldn't spring into action until George got home on account of not being able to figure out the oven.

143

"Hi, George!" I called out merrily from the kitchen as he unlocked the million locks and came through the door. "Can you get this oven to go on?" And George put a match to the oven and singed off his eyelashes and eyebrows and a good chunk of his forelock.

Monday I started drama school, rising in the morning to ride in a wad of people in a steaming subway car that more often than not stopped between stations, and arriving one hour early at the school, where it soon became apparent there wasn't a single possible guy in the group. For two hours I had to stare at myself in a leotard as we did exercises and tried to feel what it was like to be orange juice being poured into a glass, and then we had the acting classes, where I wasn't any good, not that it mattered, because I got the feeling all anyone cared about was this blonde from Texas whose parents had a lot of money. Then back I jostled onto the subway, except this time I took the 7th Ave. express, instead of the Broadway local, which landed me at 125th Street, right in the middle of Harlem. I knew something was wrong when, instead of rapid Spanish, I heard hoots and whistles as I climbed the blackened stairs out of the station, and all I could think of was what they advised us to do at Radcliffe under such circumstances: walk straight down the middle of the street with a determined air —which I did in my mini shift and platform heels to the increased appreciation of the crowds that sat on the stoops of either side of the street.

"Hey, little girl," they called out, and I tightened my lips with determination until I looked so unattractive that everyone lost interest.

"What the hell are you doing here?" asked a white cop as he hurried by, and then, finally, a black cabbie stopped.

"You look like little lost Jesus," he said and I hopped in.

That weekend George went off to Tanglewood with some friends, leaving me alone in the apartment, where you couldn't tell if it was day or night, which would have been all right if Harry had showed up as he'd promised, which he didn't, so I shoved the hamburger I'd bought him into the freezer and went off to see *Funny Girl,* finishing four candy bars before the opening credits were over, and hating, for the next two and a half hours, everyone in the audience as they howled with delight.

I moved back to the parents' the following week, and was, for the remainder of the summer, pretty nearly a joy to be with. I managed this by pretending I was a foreign exchange student. I even ate what the parents ate. Every night I would help my mother cut the vegetables and then my father would come home and we would start the cocktail hour by watching Walter Cronkite. I never drank with the parents because it was a waste of calories. The parents were very moderate and it had always driven me nuts that they had exactly two one-ounce drinks every night, but in mid-July they started skipping even these when we all went on Weight Watchers' Maintenance Diets. Whenever Eric Sevareid came on the parents listened in hushed awe. Personally, I couldn't stand the guy, but I couldn't say anything after being so liberal and getting out of all those exams. Then we would have dinner of a hearty helping of vegetables without butter and a lean piece of fish or chicken and a yellow apple for dessert. Often I would save my apple to watch a TV show at ten. I watched a lot of TV that summer, "Medical Center" being my favorite show. The TV guide always said something like "Gannon (Chad Everett) helps a pregnant diabetic cross the desert." Usually there was a girl with long hair who was dying of cancer who sang songs for the little children in the hospital, as a kind of subplot.

After dinner and my ten o'clock program I would go upstairs to smoke cigarettes in my room, which was next to the playroom, where the enormous trophy case that the parents had given Harry for his eighteenth birthday stood facing the wall. Harry had been angry the moment he'd first laid eyes on the case, with dozens of his awards gleamingly displayed on green felt shelves, and the poor parents hadn't had any choice

145

but to store it in the attic in Concord for five years, then lug it along to the house in Bedford Hills. Usually I was a little hungry by then, so I felt noble in my denial, puffing my cigarette pensively—when I was thin I could be pensive, when I was fat I was merely depressed—and watching the smoke waft over my thin legs. Technically I was not supposed to smoke cigarettes in my room, due to my father's knowing two people who burned themselves up in bed. Also, he had accidentally started a cornfield on fire when he was a little boy, and when the barn in Concord had burned down there was some talk about the smoldering coals he had left in the grill, a detail that we were not encouraged to bring up around Mr. Plucket from Mass. Mutual Life. After three or four cigarettes, I would take out the plastic record player my father had won as a commission from the Wendell Mattress Company and play Judy Collins for a while and think about Richard Townsend in a detached sort of way and go to bed.

I went up to Radcliffe a couple of days early that September, and I felt really happy as I sat in the Casablanca, where Harry had been playing since the end of summer school. He was full of energy, picking up one instrument after another and playing so magnificently one minute you could hardly stand it, and so sweetly the next, you could close your eyes and not know whether you were hearing soprano sax or clarinet or flute. Spencer was still in Switzerland, where for four thousand dollars he was learning to fly with the maharishi—really, it wasn't flying, but this kind of hop you did after hours and hours of meditating, Spencer had explained when he was in Westchester for a few days that July to buy long underwear and go to the dentist. Spencer still got treated to the dentist by the parents because they felt guilty about all the money he had saved them by not going to college. Anyway, Spencer wasn't around, so Harry was playing with Stu Craig, a jazz guitarist he'd met through Amanda Moon, the singer he'd been recording with the year before when we'd come to kidnap him. Stu had the face of an angel and beautiful chestnut brown curls, but I'd never really been interested in him—he was too old, around twenty-six. That night, though, he started giving me these long mournful stares from the stage, and when he sat down with us between sets and I learned, from some sad reference, that he was living with someone, I began to fall just a little bit in love.

"You're very pretty," said Stu, as if it hurt, and touched my hand as he dragged himself away to go home to his girl-friend Vera, who, it turned out, was about eight times better-looking than I.

I stayed at Harry's apartment in East Cambridge that night —I don't remember where Harry was, but he was off some-where and had given me the keys. I'd never even heard of East Cambridge before, and I must say, it was the dreariest place I had ever been, monotonous and hopeless, far worse than Har-lem, where at least there was fear. There was no sense of its being anywhere—no hills or dales, whatever a dale is, just flat flat flat with ramshackle three-family row houses continuing forever into the distance. Harry was sharing the apartment with Charlene, a disagreeable woman who was an astrologist and hurried in and out of the apartment wearing a sweeping black wool cape, even though it must have been about ninety-five degrees. The bathroom had no basin, so you had to brush your teeth over the kitchen sink, which was piled to the top with dirty dishes. To add to these charms, Charlene owned a ferocious Great Dane that she kept on a leash that reached all over the apartment, stopping just short of Harry's bed. Harry's mattress was bare—only an old sheet was bunched up in one corner, and when I pulled it out, it was filled with decaying dog bones—so I lay crouched at one end, still dressed in my sleeveless shift, the moon through the window bleaching out my golden tan. I thought soulfully about Stu Craig for the longest time, and then I fell asleep.

Harry never showed up the next morning, so I spent the rest of the weekend on the bed watching his television die.

The set did not break all at once, but slowly and painfully: every hour there would be a little more black at the bottom and top of the tube, squeezing the picture into the center until it was one horizontal band. I stayed with it until the end. The last night I watched Peggy and Link and the cute-looking guy whose name you can never remember put their arms around each other at the end of a "Mod Squad" rerun, all the size of a fingernail, and I was moved to tears.

Chapter Eleven

This is the dawn of a new age is the kind of remark I made to myself that September, not being one to take a cool look at things, and yet I could not help feeling as corny as a character in the books my father was always reading, when the narrator says, before everybody has to go fight World War II, "Going down for a soda . . . or to the Bijou for a movie . . . these were the best years." Suddenly I found that I was going to classes in the day and eating at mealtimes and sleeping at night as if living normally were some miraculous new discovery. Each morning shimmered with hope, even without a boyfriend, for Harry was back at Harvard with me, and anything was possible now that Harry was well.

Harry's headache was gone, even though he was in school again, and he was an intellectual once more, after so many years, all enthused about the math and philosophy courses he was taking and lugging along a pile of books with him every night when he went to play at the Casablanca. Harry was in heaven, you could tell, when he played his clear, beautiful music, this time for the first time without the agony that had always been there, buried at the bottom of his horn. He was at peace when he played, and the best thing, as Harry said, was that he could feel this way and be completely off drugs, having recently decided to stop the lithium and go it on his own. Harry said there was nothing like being clean and drug free and finding music so wonderful you couldn't seem to stop buying records and bringing them to people and saying listen to this, listen to this, it's great.

Spencer returned from Switzerland in late September, and his first night back playing at the Casablanca, he and Harry and William and I went out to the Blue Parrot between sets. The Blue Parrot was more like a glorified coffeehouse than a restaurant, and Harry spent most of the time searching the menu for something that had a sauce. Harry loved sauces; unaware of their existence for so long due to our mother's good, plain cooking, he was the only one we knew who liked the food at college, with its tan glutinous sauces, more than the food at home. Generally we never went out to dinner, but the parents had sent a check out of the blue for us to go and get some decent food, and that night we all had wine, even Spencer, who was so pure, if you don't count two packs of Camels and a new girl a day. We had a really good time at the Blue Parrot, and when Spencer and Harry went back and played, they were so loose and so natural together that everyone in the Casablanca, for those few timeless minutes, forgot to spill drinks over one another as they tried to pick each other up and instead listened to Spencer singing "What did I do . . . to be so black and blue . . . " as if his heart was breaking before their very eyes, and then they let Harry hold them in the palm of his hand as he went way off soloing on his tenor sax. You couldn't trust Harry's taste on most things, but he sure had it when it came to music. Just as you were wondering where the heck the song was, back he brought you to the melody and to Spencer, and they ended together on one long minor chord.

People were still clapping when Thumper Kohler, the manager of the bar, rushed up to the stage and dragged Harry and

Spencer into the back room and yelled at them at the top of his lungs, "You're background music, that's all you're supposed to be, do you hear me, don't ever play like that again, nobody bought a drink for forty-five minutes!" and then we heard Spencer, the only one in the family who wasn't a yeller, yelling back that Thumper was a crummy bastard and Spencer would never play there again.

Spencer kept his word after his run-in with Thumper and went back to driving his cab six nights a week in the combat zone and so it was Harry and Stu Craig I listened to those fall nights in the Casablanca. I would sit there at the front table with upturned face, and whenever Stu threw me a particularly long gaze between numbers, Harry would raise his eyebrows at me a couple of times to be sure I'd seen and to show his enthusiasm for the cause. Both William and Spencer had warned me not to get mixed up with Stu, he was up to no good, but I had discussed the matter with Harry at great length and he had approved, provided Stu broke up with Vera, which we figured would happen any day now—you only had to look at Stu when he looked at me and you knew. Stu hadn't heard the news yet that we were going out, but this did not deter Harry and me. "Think how musical your children will be," Harry marveled.

Harry and I had decided that I should major in philosophy so that we could take the same courses and argue brilliantly with each other in class. I'd gotten a great single in Daniels that fall, a corner room with picture windows looking out at the Radcliffe Quad, and Harry always dropped by in the morning to pick me up, even though Radcliffe wasn't on the way to anything, and we would head to the Yard together, me trotting alongside of him, trying to keep up, as he strode through the leaves with his long legs; it never seemed to occur to Harry that other people weren't six-foot-seven, though now I suddenly remember that Harry always made a point of liking only girls who were under five-two. "They fit perfectly with your body in bed," he had explained to the parents, who had never dreamed of wanting to know. Harry always had a couple of instruments with him in case inspiration grabbed him, and one sunny morning he put my flute together out on the steps of Mass. Hall after our Marxism class and taught Gus Horton, whom we'd spotted in class, "Twinkle, twinkle, little star."

"I knew it," Harry had said when Gus had succeeded in spitting out the tune, "he's brilliant first day" (whereas to me, whom Harry had given a lesson earlier in the week, it had been "See, even if you're tone deaf you can learn to improvise!"), and Gus had gone out that afternoon and bought a flute, and for a couple of weeks Harry and I'd regularly gone over to Gus's room after Marxism. Harry would teach while I sat on a desk, smiling away in the late morning sun, my bare legs dangling from my miniskirt, a picture that still lives in my heart: me thin, Harry happy, and Gus Horton, soon fated to fall in love with me and take me off into the sunset while both families beamed their approval. If I could return to anywhere in my past, it would be back to those uneventful, sparkling mornings, no doubt lost, if they were ever there, in Harry's and Gus's memories because nothing whatsoever really happened during them, except the hope sprang in my heart that Harry would be the star again, and as he was moving back into his rightful place in the heavens, I felt the ground coming back under me, and the bright years of our family returning.

Feeling cocky, the three of us kids went to a Harvard football game one day as a lark, Spencer in his dead man's overcoat from Goodwill, Harry in some kind of messy covering, and me, freezing but cute as a button in a tweed miniskirt and an old brown riding jacket from my mother's youth. We looked like hoboes in the stands of Wellesley girls and scarfed clubbies, as different as we had against the preppy background of our hometown, but now we were proud of being different, we wanted to stand out, because we felt that together against the multitudes we would achieve greatness.

But what my father would have wanted a snapshot of much more was a scene that took place on another Saturday, in mid-October, when, more like on a date, I went to a football game with Gil, Richard's former roommate.

Richard was taking the year off to live at home in California and learn cabinet-making—in those days everybody at Harvard was always trying to decide whether they should weave straw mats or make clay pots when they graduated, or go to law school—and I'd found I could already talk about him casually without the slightest pang. As if to put this to the test, I began to see a great deal of Gil. We had a *platonic* relationship, we agreed, and made much of the fact that we could be friends without doing anything, as if this was terribly mature. It wasn't exactly excruciatingly difficult for me not to do anything, since I hadn't done anything before, at least technically, but Gil didn't know that, for my virginity was a fact that only my father was apt to bring up at gatherings— no matter how many times my mother said she didn't think the Andrewses or the Dangles much cared, and then, how did he know, since it seemed to her that whenever she'd called me in the mornings I was always supposed to be at some seven o'clock class.

At any rate, Gil and I were lifelong friends that October, and we went to a game as an experience and sat in the stands talking away and glancing down now and then at the teams to see if they were still there. Some part of me understands most things, even the desire to murder (if I had a gun the thought would cross my mind to apply it to someone whose radio was turned up too high), but no part of me has ever understood being a spectator at athletic events, where the only activity I am engrossed in viewing is the interminably sluggish movement of the so-called clock. I had grown up believing that a girl to be feminine had to ask whatever guy was available, even if it was just some relative, what a "down" was, and always I had asked and then not listened. So it was great being

153

there with Gil, who was an intellectual and much more interested in discussing whether this actress at the Loeb might not be in love with him than in explaining to me how the first down wasn't really the first down, or whatever that hitch is, and the game was over in no time. We parted in the Square with a smile and a strengthening look.

"You're a super lady," said Gil, and I walked back to Daniels under the bluest of skies.

Still uplifted, I turned into the Radcliffe Quad, where I saw a number of leaflets littering the sidewalk and blowing across the grass. Long ago I had stopped reading handouts, but there was something about these that attracted my attention, and I grabbed at one and picked it up.

"You Can Play the Flute!" it announced in bold handwritten letters, and continued at great length below. "Music is a language. You learned to speak English (another common language) and likewise you can learn to speak (improvise) music. . . . " I was still reading what Harry had written when I walked into the dorm lobby and picked up my phone messages.

"Your brother Harry called, 12:03 P.M.," said one of the slips. "Wants to disclose plans for saving the universe."

You could have knocked me over with a feather, but this was because I am a moron. That Monday in Marxism there had been a little incident that I had managed to banish from my mind five minutes after it had happened. I'd been sitting snugly between Harry and Gus Horton, listening to Augustus Tobin talk about the withering away of the state, when out of the corner of my eye I'd noticed Harry scribbling furiously away. In that instant I'd known it was all over—it was like seeing the Mack truck in the dream the second before it hits —and my whole wonderful life had fallen with a thud to the bottom of my stomach. *Please, God, let the class end early,* I'd prayed, wondering where the hell all those fire drills were you always used to get in grade school, and then suddenly Harry had jumped up and, in front of hundreds, dashed forward to

154

the podium from which Augustus Tobin was speaking and shoved what he'd been writing in front of him. Startled, Tobin, who was a mild man, had read the note to himself, gulped, and then continued with his lecture. Harry had stood there, watching him closely, and then marched triumphantly back to his seat.

"I told him he was wrong about Marxism," he'd confided to me in a loud voice, as he sat smugly back in his chair with folded arms. "Lady Meredith Davies is going to take over the world."

After class Harry had acted as if nothing had happened, behaving so reasonably I found myself dismissing the incident as a fluke—some genes of my father's kicking in for a change —but when I got the note from Harry about saving the universe it was clear where we were headed. Except this time I didn't feel panic or desperation; I just felt a sense of calmness, as if destiny had finally reclaimed its niche and settled itself right in, cozy as could be, with no plans of moving on. With a coolness of purpose I went straight down into the basement of Daniels, put my money in the candy machine, and proceeded to down three packages of Chuckles, including the blacks. Then I went up to my room, called Spencer, and asked him where we were meeting and when. The Fellowship of the Cosmos, he replied, 289 Park Street, 5:30 P.M.—it was all very businesslike. There wasn't much time, so I applied a little blush-on, brushed my hair, and, rushing up to the Square, jumped on the Red Line to Park Street.

By now there was something about having to deal with Harry's flipping out that made me feel very competent, and I bustled down the street in a no-nonsense manner until I came to the modern office building that said Fellowship of the Cosmos out front. I clacked up the steps and into the lobby—you could hear me coming a mile away on account of these wooden clogs I had taken to wearing, which had open heels that flapped along when I hurried. The usual crowd had already assembled: the parents, Spencer, Art, William, and Uncle

Hank in from New York—Harry knew how to mobilize, you had to give him that. They were all sitting on the edge of orange plastic chairs looking nervous and not like they had a really great conversation going, and when they saw me they acted enraptured that I was there, jumping up and kissing me and making jokes about this being a reunion, and then we all sat down and began thumbing through the literature that was lying around on glass tables. Literature is a bit of an overstatement—"You too can reach Void, for just 1,200 dollars down!" headlined one article. We all felt a little silly on account of this enormous poster, which took up an entire wall, of Lady Meredith Davies' implacable face looking intently at us. Today there are all these stories about Meredith Davies having been abducted by her administrative assistants, but even back then hardly anyone ever set eyes on her in the flesh because she was living on an island in the middle of the Pacific Ocean, having been kicked out of South America or wherever it was she'd had her headquarters. Nobody of an official capacity seemed to be around, just a few ten-year-olds wearing satin space suits and glazed eyes who wandered in now and then, so I started making witty remarks about how the space kids looked as if they'd been voided of just about everything, when Harry appeared.

He looked frazzled and distracted, as if he really didn't have time for us. Whenever Harry summoned you together to disclose his plans for saving the universe, you always wanted to apologize for having interrupted him in the middle of some more important meeting. He had a large dictionary in his hands, which he opened and began to rifle through. Finally he stopped and pointed to a page.

"Aha!" he said, looking at us with great significance, "*just* as I suspected. It's no accident." And then he read aloud deliberately and with searing enunciation: "'Founder: to fill with water and sink; *said of a ship*.'" We looked at him blankly but not without interest. "Lady Meredith Davies is the *founder* of the Fellow*ship* of the Cosmos," Harry said, with some impatience. "This proves that the Fellow*ship* is going to founder and sink and I am going to take over the Cosmos and save the world." He snapped the dictionary shut as a man and a woman, dressed in gray and looking agitated, came into the lobby from the rooms beyond.

"You have to leave, you have to leave," they said hurriedly and ushered us out.

Woodward Hospital agreed to take Harry, but not until the next morning, so we all went out to dinner and got drunk, with the exception of Harry, for whom drinking would have been superfluous. Harry was pretty amusing in the light of a million glasses of wine, and everyone had a grand old time, except for the waitress, who Harry maintained had been Bambi's mother in another life.

"You shouldn't have died and left that damn deer all by himself," he growled when she brought him the cheeseburger.

Harry spent the night in a HoJo motel room, guarded by Uncle Hank, William, and Spencer. There were two double beds in the room, and Spencer said he had dreaded sleeping next to Harry who, even with your eyes closed, you could tell was sleeping with his mouth open. But he didn't have to worry, because Harry kept them up all night referring ominously to his plans for the world, though never quite getting to the plans themselves, only William managing, as always, to keep up his end of the conversation, with Spencer braving it out in the real world for chips and Coca-Colas during breaks. The next morning the four of them went over to Woodward Hospital. Spencer said two big muscley aides had spotted them marching down the street and, giving them an alarmed appraisal, rushed back inside the hospital, returning with four more aides. Harry, of course, gave them no fight.

I couldn't visit Harry until the next day on account of moving up to Harvard. Three of us were exchanging our singles in Daniels for a suite at Leverett House and, because the whole thing was illegal, we had to get it done fast. They were allowing a limited number of Cliffies to live at Harvard that

157

year, and it was all based on a lottery in which I had picked the second to last number. Then I had run across these pimply guys who had a suite in Leverett but wanted to live at Radcliffe and hang around the dorm kitchen Saturday nights, hoping to get lucky, I guess, and within hours I'd rounded up two other girls with singles, and so up we went the next day hauling our suitcases and linen along Mount Auburn Street, only to be caught at the gate by the master of Leverett House.

"This is totally wrong," he said, dutifully but without bureaucratic conviction, as he met us clutching our pillows, "but now you're here, you're here, I suppose," and then he walked on.

By four that afternoon I had moved everything in and was hanging my watercolor of the boy playing his saxophone to the girl in the house over my bed, which I'd figured would make a good conversation piece. Our suite was on the ground floor and had a big living room with a fireplace and then a long hallway with a bathroom and four bedrooms coming off it. Though they had high ceilings, the bedrooms were cell-like, and I missed my loft, which the guy who was taking my old room was actually tearing down. Spencer had come up with the sleeping loft idea when he'd come back from learning to fly in Switzerland—I don't think there was any connection —and he had built himself one in the illegal apartment he was renting in a run-down building in the financial district. The building was zoned only commercially and the heat went off at night and you had to use the rest rooms down the hall, but Spencer had made his room really nice, sanding the floors and painting the walls white, and hanging pictures of the maharishi beaming benignly down everywhere you looked.

Still, I loved my new room. I put my bed next to the window, which faced the courtyard. Wherever you looked you saw boys coming and going in the fall leaves. I sat against my window ledge in the late afternoon sun and gazed out, smoking cigarettes and sighing with happiness. The only thing that nagged at me was the fact that Leverett House was full of jocks —Adams House, which was full of theater types, was where one really wanted to be—but, I thought to myself philosophically, you couldn't have everything.

William came by after supper and told me about taking Harry to the hospital and all, and then I pulled out a bottle of cheap sherry and we discussed girls for him and boys for me, forcing the sticky liquor down our throats as if it was medicine. William had worked in a meat packing plant that summer to further the Marxist cause, but he had been fired for talking too much and not getting enough boxes done or something, and now was making the transition from radicalism to alcoholism with his usual grace.

"How old are you, Lizzie?" William asked as part of a never-ending joke about how he just couldn't believe I was no longer the twelve-year-old girl wearing the white polished sneakers and sparkly blue glasses I'd been Harry's first day at Harvard, when all the parents and William and Harry and I had stood awkwardly around the room in Wigglesworth, when the world had been so bright with hope.

"I'm nineteen, you know very well," I told him.

"You can't be nineteen," said William, "I know *girls* who are nineteen."

The next morning I went over to visit Harry. Woodward was semiprivate so it wasn't quite as depressing as Boston Rehab. The day room looked less like a Greyhound bus station and more like a high school cafeteria, where, instead of turkey fricassee and peanut-buttered bread, you were offered black-and-white TVs that sat on plastic trays along the wall. The room was large and had rows of tables with Formica tops designed, presumably by someone who got paid for it, to remind you of coarse woven cloth. When I walked in, I saw Harry sitting by himself, calm as could be. He wasn't on any drugs and he seemed completely normal—nothing like the other patients, lifeless and looking bleakly into space—and suddenly I thought, *He's done it, somehow he's pulled himself into cogency, away from all this.* Whether it was real or a con job, I had to admire his spirit.

"Let's go in here," he said and beckoned to me and we went into a small glass office and sat down as if we were two lawyers wrapping up a deal. "I'm leaving today," Harry informed me. "They can't keep me here unless I sign myself in," and, as it turned out, he was absolutely right.

Harry was very reasonable as counsel for his defense. He said he knew he had a few problems, but he certainly wasn't crazy, and his theory was that it was hospitals that made you crazy—remember what had happened with the Thorazine. I remembered, and I looked at Harry's clear eyes and steady hands and I wondered if all along Harry had been right—that the hospitals did make things worse, that we'd done a terrible, terrible thing when we'd kidnaped him and locked him in Boston Rehab. In the middle of Harry's arguments, Dr. Atwood came in and asked me if I would like to speak with him in *his* office. Dr. Atwood was a tall, handsome man with pure-black hair who had roomed with my father at Princeton and broken the hearts of a hundred girls (who, in his wake, had called my mother at two in the morning sobbing), before he'd finally married at forty. The parents had asked his help when they'd found out Boston Rehab wouldn't take Harry back. Dr. Atwood confirmed what Harry had found out so rapidly, that since he was over twenty-one he either had to sign himself in or had to be deemed so crazy that he was a menace to society, which at the moment he clearly was not. Atwood had talked to the parents and explained that the only other option was going to court to have him committed. Cousin Dee Dee's husband had gone to court once, after Dee Dee'd buried the silver tea service against Girondist attack, and it had been a painful, humiliating experience, and the parents couldn't bear to do it to Harry, who had once stood so tall.

160

Dr. Atwood was a kind, contented man who smoked a pipe and talked with a low resonance, measuring each word. "Lizzie," he said, pausing, as if to let the fact of my name sink in, and then continued, "Harry must learn that he cannot be crazy and function in the real world."

The theory that the parents and Dr. Atwood had come up with was that if they let him out, Harry would soon recognize his helplessness and come running back to the arms of Woodward Hospital. My theory was, if Harry came to live with me, I could make him better. The shrinks had been so stupid at Boston Rehab, and then Harry had once said—admittedly after discussing for three straight hours one afternoon at his apartment whether some girl walking by him on the street had smiled at him or not—that there were some matters he could only talk to me about, that somehow I understood things, even though I was a virgin. And I knew, even before Harry had recognized my little sister existence as anything more than a mosquito buzzing around his head, always I had known, as I'd watched Harry stride across the street with his cross-guard belts X-ed across his chest or up to the podium to receive one of his innumerable trophies, that no one could appreciate Harry as I could. And, while we had all worshiped him in his glory, in his suffering I had come to love him more than myself, and I realized, at Woodward that day, that I didn't need Harry to be the star again for me, or for my other brothers or for the parents. I wanted it again for Harry, for I knew suddenly that he had to have it, that, for some reason beyond me, Harry could never be happy unless he was perfect in our eyes, that he would never believe we could love him unless he was wonderful and invincible and shining.

That afternoon in Woodward I decided that no one could help him as I could, not the shrinks, not the parents, not the drugs. They weren't going to stuff him full of insecticide again and plant him on a chair to watch the clock—I wouldn't let them, I would make him brownies again, just as I used to

161

when I was vying with Mother and the canned fruit cocktail, and I would let him talk and talk, until the birds began to sing or however long it took, I didn't care, and then he would be better, I knew he would be better.

It was an interesting concept, all in all, but not one I was inclined to share with Dr. Atwood, and not one I rushed to the phone to impart to the parents, who were probably that afternoon sitting in the sunken living room in Bedford Hills grimly telling each other that they had done the right thing.

Instead, I excused myself from Dr. Atwood and went back to Harry's office to explain my plan, and then we made a deal. He could live with me if he obeyed the rules: he could play at the Casablanca every night if he wanted, but he had to be back in bed by midnight; he had to eat three meals a day, which I would be happy to bring him on a tray from the dining hall; and he had to tell me everywhere he was going. I hadn't had a clue what the rules would be until they dropped decisively from my mouth, and yet, as I voiced each one calmly and clearly, I felt surer and surer that all was under control, that nothing could stop us now, that forward we were going on to victory.

Harry was very appreciative and cooperative. He told me he'd known all along I would help, that I was the only one who would understand. "I'll do anything you say," he promised, in that accommodating way everyone has when they've just gotten their way, against all odds.

After conferring, lyingly, with Dr. Atwood, Harry and I took a series of broken-down trolleys and went over to his apartment in East Cambridge to pick up his instruments, which, it turned out, weren't there. Harry had hocked them earlier that week in order to be able to donate more money to the Fellowship of the Cosmos, with the result that, his means of livelihood gone, he now had *no* money to give to anybody. So we went over to the pawnshop and Harry brought out his Mastercharge and we took the trolleys and instruments back to Leverett House and settled Harry into the extra cubicle, next to Merrill's.

Merrill was one of the roommates I had dug up to make the switch from Radcliffe to Harvard. Her mother was a famous artist and her father a big diplomat and she had lived in Europe most of her life, attending Swiss boarding schools and English boarding schools, with the result that she went around barefoot straight through the winter, quoting Proust and singing Wagner at the top of her lungs, or, when she got modern, "She loves you, hey, hey, hey!" I had never met anyone like Merrill before; in Concord if you were cultural you went over to Thoreau Street to eat at A Different Drummer, where the menu was partly in French. Harry and Merrill had got on like a house afire from the moment they'd met the week before—sitting around on the floor of my room in Daniels arguing furiously about Hegel and Sartre and jumping up and playing each other records as if to prove a point, with Harry picking up his sax now and then to pitch in and give *Die Meistersinger* a hand. Merrill was passionate and effusive about everything, and only Merrill would have reacted to her roommate's moving in a brother fresh from the looney bin with enthusiasm.

The extra cubicle had only a bed and a desk and its walls were a Crest-colored green, but I did my best to make it seem cozy by moving things around. The only poster I could find was the guy screaming in the tunnel, which wasn't particularly heartwarming, and I couldn't part with the watercolor of the girl in the house, so I moved in a bunch of my brightest textbooks to give the room color and took the clipping from the *Harvard Crimson* that said "Life is one damn thing after another" that I had thought was so hilarious and pinned it on Harry's door to add a humorous touch.

Harry was very sweet and docile, probably because he hadn't had any sleep in a week, and he agreed to go to bed that night at ten. He must have thanked me a dozen times as I found him a toothbrush and packed him off to the bathroom, and I

163

felt such a rush of warmth and peace inside that I didn't know what to say or do, so I went to get him an extra blanket and the little light from my desk in case he wanted to read the Nietzsche book I'd found for him before he went to sleep. Then Stu Craig happened to come by and together we gave Harry a couple of Sominex and, with the pride of new parents, tucked him in.

Stu lived near Radcliffe and had been happening by my room in Daniels every day since September—usually he was on his way to throw a Frisbee in the Radcliffe Quad and in too much of a hurry to even sit down. The air between us had always been filled with meaningfulness, with Stu darting me wrenching glances every two seconds, but nothing had ever been said, except by Spencer who, when he was present, would ask Stu pointedly, whenever he could get it in, "How's Vera?" Unlike Harry, Spencer got very moral on me about Stu Craig, even after Stu had spent an entire day helping Spencer build me my loft.

"I think you should save yourself till the right guy comes along," Spencer had lectured me that evening, after waiting and waiting for Stu to leave. "Look at me; I haven't gone out with a girl for two years."

"What about the ones you're always sleeping with?" I had asked. "Last week there were four."

"Come on, Lizzie," Spencer had said, "those don't count."

But Harry had continued rooting for Stu and me and a camaraderie had sprung up among the three of us. It was only natural on that night, after we softly closed the door on Harry, who was already drifting off, that Stu took me gently into his arms and gave me a long, sweet kiss, and it was at that moment that I knew that we understood each other, that it was inevitable that we would be as one, that it was time to open our hearts to the fact that we shared a bond that nothing could break—but as usual, I was dressing things up a bit.

Chapter Twelve

I woke up at four the next morning to the sound of Harry forcefully spelling "Pa-ci-fic O-cean" at the end of, as my phone bill was later to inform me, a two-and-a-half-page telegram to Lady Meredith Davies.

"Harry?" I whispered as I stumbled down the hall. He gestured impatiently at me to be quiet as he finished the address and then hung up the phone.

"Dig ya later," he said and, swinging his instruments under his arms, walked out the front door.

I watched the heavy door slam softly shut and walked into the dark living room, where Merrill was sitting on the couch. It turned out that while I'd been sleeping like a baby, Harry and Merrill had been carrying on a spirited discussion concerning the nature of existence, with a side argument on why Merrill should drop everything and go with Harry to the Loire Valley.

"The thing is," Merrill said breathlessly when I dropped down next to her, "I think he makes sense," and she went on to try to describe their conversation, all about beingness and reincarnation and a tad or two about Lady Meredith Davies, but of course she soon realized she couldn't make head nor tail of it.

"Oh, I don't know," she sighed finally, tossing her passport onto the couch, "but it made sense, it really did." The truth was, Harry had a grandiose and impassioned view of life when he was high, and if you allowed yourself to jump onto the bandwagon of his logic, it was all very alluring, though later you could never quite remember what the point had been.

"Face it," I said philosophically, "Harry's nuts. Let's go to breakfast."

Merrill was sloppy and overweight from giving up smoking and wore any old thing she found on the floor, and that morning she looked like she'd spent the night on a park bench, with tangled hair and great circles of mascara under her luminous eyes. She followed me into the bathroom and watched me in the mirror as I painstakingly tied on one of the long silk paisley scarves I'd taken to wearing that fall, pulling my hair back so that nobody could miss the fact that my face was so thin it almost had cheekbones, then knotting it on the side so that it streamed prettily down my tight little sweater.

"I suppose you're what they call cute," she observed clinically, viewing me as an American type, and then out we went for our assault on the dining hall, passing Linda, our other new roommate, dozing peacefully in her bed. Linda was a large, bovine blonde who had lots of nocturnal boyfriends you never seemed to meet. She was out most of the night, but during the day you could view the body lying in state on her bed, surrounded by bottles of nail polish, her large chest rising and falling rhythmically, as the clock alarm continued its gentle buzzing and the radio played Judy Collins singing "Suzanne takes you down, to a place by the river."

Merrill's face was still the face of a believer, and as I gazed at it over my coffee cups of yogurt that morning, I recalled wistfully my own former dreams. How I had pictured long sunny afternoons of Harry and me talking about life, thoughtfully, even sadly, and yet with a cozy sense of understanding.

166

"Yes, Lizzie, I see what you mean," Harry was to have said, nodding at the revelation. "Life is like that. I feel much better now that we have talked." The afternoons were to have been followed by nights in the Casablanca, where Harry played brilliantly with Stu Craig, who, freed now from Vera, held my hand across a table between sets. Perhaps upon my finger glistened an engagement ring, I cannot say. Then back Harry and I would head to Leverett House—Stu going his separate way, for now, realizing it was the brother who needed me most and loving the sister only more for such devotion—where Harry would sleep soundly through the night like a newborn who has finally learned how.

But this was not to be. Instead, Harry arrived back at the room three days later wearing a brand-new three-piece suit and carrying a shiny leather briefcase full of an enormous variety of vitamin pills, which, with a sense of urgency, he proceeded to strew all over the suite.

"It's lumps in the back," Harry explained to Merrill and me as he snapped the briefcase shut. "All my problems stem from these three lumps in my back. I found a great chiropractor in L.A. He's a fucking genius." And then he presented me with a stack of jazz records—Coltrane, Monk, etc.—upon whose covers he had carefully inserted his name with a tiny caret in the list of musicians.

As Harry seized a *Harvard Crimson* and, zealously crossing out a headline, scribbled one of his own, the final spade of dirt fell on my hopes, and I began to suspect that I was already out of my league, that there was no way I was ever going to reach Harry, who didn't even seem to know, or care, that I was present. I almost wished Harry was depressed so I could at least get him to listen to me for a minute. But he was so determinedly going about his business, filled with energy, and bustling around with no time to spare, and when he finally looked at me, his eyes were fogged, as if he was only pretending to see me, having forgotten his glasses. So, instead of the warm, understanding way I had planned to be—never judg-

167

ing, simply being there—I assumed a stern demeanor to convey what I wished was true, that I was totally in charge and knew exactly what I was doing—finding on my mouth an expression that came straight off my mother's face.

"Harry, you are crazy, and you must learn that you cannot live crazy in society," I said in an even voice, grasping desperately, after all this, at Atwood's formula.

"Dig ya later," Harry replied, and off he went to hop on a train to Grand Central Terminal, where, I was soon to learn, if you knew the exact hour of your birth, you could get a seven-page horoscope.

Harry was busy as could be the next few weeks, what with traveling back and forth to the chiropractor in L.A. and racking up hundreds and hundreds of dollars on his Mastercharge, which the Cambridge Cooperative Bank had never revoked even when his address the year before had been Boston Mental Rehabilitation Center. Cambridge Cooperative, with whom I was later to have many bitter words over my paltry bill, didn't seem to mind that Harry never once paid them a penny or that he was stark-raving mad. Harry sauntered about Harvard Square that fall dispensing lavish gifts to any person he happened to meet. It got so whenever I saw someone carrying a bundle with a puzzled expression I would turn around and walk rapidly in the other direction, and still, as I came up to the door of I-entry at Leverett House, I would end up running into the girl to whom Harry had proposed and given two wheels of Brie cheese. She was tall and gawky and when I'd spotted her hovering uncertainly about the entrance, I'd had my suspicions and tried to hurry by.

"Excuse me," she began as I ventured to slip past her, "do you live in I-entry?"

"No, no," I said, "no!"

"Oh," she sighed, with such disappointment in her voice that I was forced to listen to the whole story anyway.

Harry never slept a single wink all month. Every night I left the little light on by his bedside in case he came in late,

168

and every morning I turned it off. He was seldom home for long when he did show up, using the suite as a kind of drop for the things he'd accumulated during the day, and half the time he appeared it was five in the morning or so and I was asleep. Usually he'd run into Linda, who never returned before dawn, or Merrill, whose troubled intellectuals and grubby street people usually crawled away before the rising sun, and the next morning I would hear reports from them about how, instead of panhandling, Harry had stood in the Square giving away nickles and dimes (which nobody had taken, figuring it had to be some trick), or how a robber had accosted Harry at two in the morning in the Cambridge Common and held him at gunpoint while Harry patiently explained all the various reasons why he himself needed his watch, which wasn't worth much anyway, until the guy had shrugged and walked away, or how Harry had talked nonstop at Linda even as she got in bed and fell sound asleep. Sometimes nobody was there when Harry dropped by, and he'd leave behind a complete set of Wagner or a map of the stars with our various astrological signs arrowed and circled—just to say hi.

As for the theory that Harry couldn't live crazy in society, I gave up expecting old society to lend a hand after the night I found him pounding away on the concert piano they kept locked up at Adams House. How he got in there I will never know, but when I heard the racket as I was walking down Quincy Street— piano was the one instrument Harry couldn't play—I knew it was Harry. It was midnight and I ran into Adams House two strides ahead of the night watchman, his hand on his holster. *Well,* I thought to myself, wincing for the blow, *I guess this is it.* Harry banged both hands on the keyboard and stood up.

"You're fired!" he cried out hotly, and the night watchman skulked away.

I had known upon the first mention of bumps on the back that I would not be able to save Harry, but now it began to dawn on me that nobody else would be able to, either—that he might just go on and on, mad in the streets forever. So on those occasions when I did encounter him, frenzied and barking out illogic to no one in particular, I felt the dull pounding of despair and had to look away. And yet, there was no next step to take. I couldn't betray him by calling Atwood or the parents, because I couldn't bear to see him again bound by tranquilizers, no longer himself, for as awful as his madness was, at least he was Harry, filled with the power to obtain a Mastercharge he didn't deserve and to fire a night watchman in a building he had no right to be in, Harry, still free and soaring, however close to skidding on the ground. I almost felt it would be better for him to crash in a blaze of glory than sizzle out in a mental hospital, without dignity or any semblance of self.

As for Stu Craig, who I had hoped would be my salvation, he was coming over a lot less often, usually at night and only when Harry was in L.A. or New York. Gone were the Frisbees and the long romantic looks, and in their place was a seamy thrashing about. You might say I wasn't exactly holding my breath waiting for Stu to break the news of our love to old Vera, and yet I could not shake the belief that our hearts beat as one, that we were meant to be—although now that I think of it there were some lapses in my own commitment, considering that it was during this month that I managed to kiss twenty-nine men, or boys, as we called them then. It was a number that strained the bounds of delicacy, admittedly, but then I needed something on a dramatic scale to keep my mind off Harry, and the study of college boys was the only academic field that had ever claimed my full attention. Whether I'm counting Stu Craig in the twenty-nine I can't begin to know, but I do believe that the figure is accurate because what mattered at the time was quantity, constant change keeping up with the frantic tempo Harry had introduced into our lives, and I kept track of it all in a journal I'd started. The journal-writing was inspired by Anaïs Nin, but I cannot say her entries much resembled mine, which on a given day might read:

170

"Lunch: 2 yogurts, one plate collard greens, 2 Tootsie Pops; Dinner: 3 bowls cottage cheese. Kissed T.F. outside H-entry." It was generally at lunch that I would select my victim, or sometimes at dinner, depending on when I got inspired. I usually got inspired after I received a bill from the phone company for one of Harry's telegrams to the middle of the Pacific Ocean or found, sticking on the bottom of my shoe, one of Harry's giant globular vitamin pills, after which I would flounce into the dining hall in a giddy mood, accompanied by Merrill, who was always up for anything and once jumped up on a table and did a belly dance. In the beginning of our roommateship, Merrill had kind of embarrassed me, ruining it when a couple of vaguely cute guys would sit down next to us by quoting Proust at them, but after Harry came to live with us, it became harder and harder to be embarrassed by anything.

"Move your head a little more to your right," I would say to Merrill when she blocked my view. "I'm in love."

As a rule, I would pick out two or three guys to increase my odds, or even four when the choices were particularly ambitious and I felt I needed a safety. I would happen to meet up with them at the Leverett House Grill or in the dinner line, or on bolder days I would invite them to a party at the room. William and I were rather prone to giving parties at the room that month when there weren't any other parties to go to.

I'm sure these relationships were quite meaningful for the few hours they lasted, but I must say, my mind grows dim when I try to remember specific faces. There was a tall black guy who was trying to give up white girls, and two or three from the group who wore rags and were always borrowing money to go to the movies and later got trust funds of one million dollars. There was the boy with the goatee who made me stare with him at the fish in his aquarium and told me his roommates thought I was a narc because I didn't smoke pot. Then there was the really handsome guy who had played Oc-

171

tavius Caesar who, I somehow got wind of, had given up acting to do Zen. He had become skinnier and even more aloof than he'd been the year before, but I managed to run across him at the yogurt table and have a conversation about how all my life I had been attracted to the Eastern religions, and by the next morning I was sitting with him and another believer in a shed on the Charles and doing some sort of deep breathing for about an hour. Actually, it was only I who clocked in at an hour, leaving them inhaling in the freezing shed, where for all I know they are still today. Then there was a senior who had a disgusting glob-light device you were supposed to admire, and there was even a jock. Jocks were against my principles, but when you're dealing in quantity you have to make exceptions. The funny thing was, the jock ended up being the only one out of the whole lot to maintain any lingering feeling for me. I met up with him in the grill a few weeks after our encounter and I didn't know him from Adam. The lights were dim and he was pretty drunk and he came up to me and blubbered how I had ruined his life and why didn't I like him anymore? I tried to dredge up some feeling for him, at the same time searching my memory for his name, but there was nothing to be found on either count. I remember thinking, *This is how Richard Townsend probably felt when you snuffed that you loved him, why didn't he love you.* I said I was sorry as nicely as I could, but when he dissolved into real sobbing, I felt it was better to leave. As I walked through the courtyard I was feeling kind of bad, thinking how maybe I'd better slow down and all, and then when I opened the door to the suite, there was Harry.

He was squatting on the floor of the living room, holding a pack of cards and flipping them over intently one at a time. You couldn't help being drawn into figuring out what he was doing, and I stood on the threshold mesmerized; I don't know if Harry realized I was there, but I got the feeling it wouldn't have made a whole lot of difference. His face grew tense with concentration as he drew from the top of the deck.

"Eight!" Harry said vehemently as he flipped the card, which was a five of clubs, and then continued to the next card, forging onward, not allowing a ten of diamonds or two of spades to dampen his spirits, until finally an eight turned up and he pointed to it victoriously.

"See?" he announced witheringly, as if the whole world had doubted him. At the end of the deck he had four eights lined up in a row.

"Just as I predicted: four eights," Harry said, catching his breath. "I win again."

"But, Harry," I said, rousing myself at last, "you can't lose!"

"The perfect game," Harry returned, and then he presented me with his ten-page rule book he'd folded up out of lined paper, which included a chapter called "Variations on the Game."

"Try 'Nines' or even 'Jacks,'" it advised. "Use your imagination!"

I went into my bedroom and locked the door. I'd had William put a bolt on it a few weeks earlier after Harry had threatened to kill me if I ever put him in the hospital again. Now, through with his card game, Harry stood outside the door shouting, "You kidnapped me! You kidnapped me! Don't you ever kidnap me again!"

"I have no intention of kidnapping you, Harry," I called out wearily. "Go to bed." Of course I knew Harry would never harm me—he had never so much as raised his hand—but throwing the bolt was a good excuse for me to get some peace and quiet. I hadn't gotten a whole lot of sleep since Harry had moved in—if it wasn't Harry, it was the boyfriends and the parties with William, and if it wasn't the boyfriends or the parties, Merrill and I would get in a taxi in the middle of the night and go to Chez Wong's for chow mein, a ritual we'd become fond of after Harry had lost his Mastercharge trying to charge a whore with it in Chinatown.

It had all been fast and furious and rather fun in the beginning, but now things began to feel desperate and decadent, and I knew the bottom had been hit a couple of nights after the Eights game when Merrill came into my room with a dead face and told me about William. He had shown up at the suite earlier that evening when I was out kissing one of my boyfriends or something, and there had been Merrill, disheveled as usual, sitting on the floor in black-bottomed bare feet swooning over some indecipherable opera she had full-blast on the record player. Merrill had always violently disapproved of William for his total lack of black consciousness, and William could never stand Merrill, with all her accents and intellectual gobbledygook, but since there was nothing else to do they took a bottle of Merrill's brandy and went out for a ride in William's decrepit Mercedes—it was as if Harry's manic energy had infected them, too, and they had to keep the party going or they would crash. Both knew of the other's dislike, and they'd sat in the car in some godforsaken place drinking the brandy from the bottle and trying to say things that wouldn't grate on each other's nerves, until finally Merrill had suggested in a hopeless sort of way, "Shall we?" and William had said why not, and they'd made love, mechanically and drearily, not even bothering to get out of the bucket seats in the front and into the back, hoping, Merrill told me grayly, it might do something for them that the booze had not.

It was about this time, too, that the parents figured out Harry was living with me. The story we'd come up with was that he was back in his apartment in East Cambridge, and when the parents had called looking for him, I'd said, "Gee, he happens to be here right now" or "Can I take a message?" but shortly after the Eights incident I got a call from Dr. Atwood. I remember thinking it was just like the parents not to call me directly but to sic some expert on me, but to tell the truth, I was at a point where I could stand some advice.

"Lizzie?" said Atwood over the phone, in the deep bass that had been such a welcome addition years before to my father's and brothers' rendition of "Side by Side." "Your father and mother have indicated that Harry is at present residing with you at your dormitory," etc., etc., taking about an hour to say I had to kick Harry out of my room. But I didn't mind; I hung on the phone remembering old Atwood in his tiger hat at my father's twenty-fifth Princeton reunion and wishing for that weekend back when I was eleven and swimming in pools at midnight with the older kids was about all you could ever ask for in life.

"Let him see, Lizzie," he repeated, "let him see that he can't live in the real world," and I said, "Yes, Dr. Atwood, I will let him see," and finally we said good-bye.

Spencer was off on Martha's Vineyard meditating with this woman and her three kids, and I hadn't dared talk to William since his night with Merrill, so I had to kick Harry out by myself. I don't know why it was so hard. It wasn't as if he'd really been living with me; he'd never come around except to bang about with his instruments and latest theories and then bang out again, and it wasn't as if I'd been able to help him or convince him he needed help or even get him to eat a double coleslaw from Elsie's. Harry hadn't really even talked to me the whole time he was supposed to be living with me—it could have been anyone at whom he spouted his crazy ideas or threw two dozen new sport shirts freshly charged at the Prep Shop. I wasn't getting anywhere with Harry, that was for certain, but Harry was getting somewhere all right, he was getting higher and higher, not in the energized way I'd seen before but reeling way up there like when you're drunk and suddenly it hits you that you're completely out of control but it's too late and you keep getting drunker. I didn't want Harry back at some slummy hospital slugged with drugs for the rest of his life and I didn't want Harry out all by himself on the city streets, lurching around like a crazy vagrant, no place to lie down but an alley floor. But I didn't know what to do any longer, so I listened to the experts, and the next day I told Harry he had to leave.

175

I was sitting on the couch facing the fireplace filled with cigarette butts when Harry swung through the front door into the living room and deposited his instruments and packages onto the chewed-up sideboard next to Merrill's whiskey, and I didn't even wait for him to finish clicking open his briefcase.

"You have to leave, Harry."

Harry said he didn't care, he didn't need me, I was a fucking hunk of meat.

"You have to leave," I said again, not so much cool this time as dead.

"'You have to leave, you have to leave,'" Harry mimicked me as he might have done when we were little, had he ever paid any attention to me then.

"Harry," I interrupted, but he shouted me down.

"Big Lizzie! Big Lizzie!" he repeated over and over, trying to make a joke of it, trying to believe he didn't believe it, but crying the whole time. I was surprised to see him cry; it was the first time I'd broken through his high and the first time he'd seemed to listen to what I had to say. But it was too late; I was kicking Harry out.

"You think you're so big, well, see if I care, see if I care, do you hear me?" Harry screamed, his face puffy now, his lips pressed down as he fought back a sob. I started to go to him, but he motioned me back.

"Go away," he screamed, "I don't want you." So I sat lifelessly back down on the couch and watched him gather his instruments and clothes. With so little sleep he was slumped over, and he hauled his body around, dragging one leg behind him. He'd hurt it doing God knows what God knows where, but I hadn't realized how bad it was until I saw him limp out. The front door shut and I sat there in the living room smoking cigarettes and staring at the fireplace until morning.

I guess what Harry did the next few days was to wander around the Square; I know he didn't go to L.A. or anywhere distant, because at least once a day he'd wander into the suite, circle once around the living room, and wander out again.

"You have to leave," I would say mechanically, but I hadn't needed to because Harry would be out the door almost as soon as he arrived.

The third night after I'd kicked him out I went over to the Casablanca, where Harry was still playing with Stu Craig. It is something of a miracle that he was able to play professionally when he was so crazy, but in some ways it was the best I ever heard him. Everything that was going on inside seemed to come screaming out of Harry's horns, and it was painful and wrenching and powerful and magnificent. Even the drunk clubbies in their tuxedos fell silent, their hearts stopped, to hear Harry play.

When I arrived that night it was between sets and the juke box was blaring and glasses were clinking and Harry was just lying there, stretched out across the small stage like a slain bear—he never slept, but had a way of resting without quite losing consciousness. Stu Craig was sitting on the edge of the platform, talking to some girl. Though it had finally penetrated my thick skull that there were other girls that Stu was helplessly attracted to besides me and the languishing beauty at home, still, if you'd asked me I would have told you I went over to the Casablanca that night to see Stu Craig. At the front table were William and Spencer, who had just gotten back from the Vineyard—"So what's new?" he'd asked innocently, when he'd called the day before. I was wearing my red crushed velvet cocktail dress, short and clinging as could be against my body, and yellow maryjanes, all for Stu Craig, but at the sight of Spencer I burst into tears.

"I don't like to see you cry," Spencer said in a quiet, reprimanding voice.

"I don't fucking care what you like, look at him lying up there!" I said.

"Lizzie, you know, it's very unattractive when you talk like that!"

"Fuck you!" I said. "Where the fuck have you been, anyway?" And then Spencer told me to calm down and started going on and on in a patient way about how we'd agreed we had no choice but to let Harry come to his own realizations, and so on, although how *we'd* agreed to all this when Spencer had been walking the sands with some thirty-five-year-old woman at the time would have been an interesting point to debate, had I not been standing in the front of the club crying so hard. I was pretty unhappy all right, and yet in the back of my mind the whole time was the dim hope that maybe Stu Craig would swoop down from the stage and take me away from it all. He was such a great hero type, too, with his dark shining curls and cherubic face, but, instead of coming to my rescue, he changed his position ever so slightly so that as he talked to the girl he was looking away from me—it was when he moved that I knew he had seen me—and it was William who saved me.

"There are two people's mental healths at stake here," said William rising, "and I'm opting for Lizzie's." The next thing I knew Spencer was also on his feet, and they were both lifting Harry off the stage and dragging him out the door. I wasn't sure where they were taking him and I was too exhausted to wonder. All I knew was that it was all over.

Later that night I found myself at a very hip party at Amanda Moon's Dana Street apartment. Amanda Moon was an intense girl who had been around Cambridge forever and sang only bitter songs, although what she was belly-aching about when her rich father bankrolled her every project was beyond me. Mostly it was a bunch of musicians milling about —you could tell who were the musicians because they all had bad posture and wore colored T-shirts and black jeans. I don't know how I got there; I must have tagged along after Joey Finkelstein, whom I'd met once through Spencer, because he was the only one of the lot there I knew to speak to. Spencer and Joey had been at Brookhill together, and Spencer had told me how the first day he met Joey, Joey had tapped him on the shoulder and dragged him off into some empty shrink's office and said, listen to this, listen to this, and then proceeded to play "When you wish upon a star . . . makes no difference who you are!" on the guitar. Spencer said he remembered thinking what kind of a nut is this guy, and then of course Joey became famous and "When You Wish Upon a Star" became the big song with which he started all his concerts. Joey was looking pretty cute that night, but he disappeared almost as soon as we got there, and though the only other person I knew to talk to was Stu Craig, he still wouldn't look me in the face. Then Amanda Moon came up to me. I'd never actually seen her before because the time we kidnapped Harry she was recording in the back studio, but instantly I knew it was she. She was little and white-blond and wearing the exact same yellow maryjanes as I was and the exact same brass sun earrings. She looked me deeply in the eye.

"Stu is very special," she said knowingly, and, to borrow my father's favorite expression, I would *of* liked to throw up.

I learned the next day that Spencer and William had taken Harry to Stillman, the infirmary at Harvard. Stillman wasn't a real hospital, just a place where students were always getting tested for VD, and never having it, or trying to get a note that said they were too sick or too screwed up to take an exam. William said they made rather a splash when they showed up with Harry around one, when things had long ago settled down into peace and quiet. The receptionist was probably saying to herself, "Well, *this* is easy," when Harry burst in with Spencer and William. Harry had woken up, to say the least, on the way over, and he hadn't been in the lobby a minute before he was accusing the poor receptionist of violating his Constitutional rights.

"You are violating Article 13, Amendment 4, of the Constitution of the United States of America," he shouted at her, and then began to sing "America, the Beautiful" with great dramatic irony. By the time the campus police arrived, Harry was threatening to transcend his body. It was at this point that one conscientious hospital aide remembered you were supposed to take away the disturbed patient's belt. For some reason they always take the belt away, I don't know why—it must be something they teach you in hospital aide school. At any rate, the aide, who was a skinny little guy, kind of slipped over and weasled Harry's belt off him while he was too busy transcending his body to notice. When Harry finally realized what had happened, he stomped after the aide, who fled to a corner of the lobby.

"I demand my belt back," shouted Harry in a menacing voice, and I'm sure the aide would have been more than happy to return it had he been able to move. Then Harry rose mightily to his full height and pointed an arm at his trembling adversary.

"Arrest that man!" Harry commanded, and, with a surety of purpose, three campus police jumped the aide.

Chapter Thirteen

Harry spent one night at Stillman, and then he was whisked back to Woodward Hospital, where for two weeks he kept up a lively banter with a black-and-white TV set.

"You'll never amount to anything!" he warned the set, and, I suppose, he had a point. The strange thing was, the whole time Harry was at Woodward, he never came down, even though they were pumping him full of Thorazine. He was scared to, I think, and then you couldn't exactly tell him how great it was going to be.

I went over every day to take Harry his mail. Harry received huge amounts of junk mail at my address—brochures from the Friends of the Volunteer Ambulance Corps, the Florida Fruit Growers, etc.—and he would leaf through each item as if it was an important state document. More interesting, however, were the personal letters Harry kept receiving from Lady Meredith Davies. I was dying to see what my pal Meredith was writing, what with all Harry's threatening telegrams to respond to, but Harry was very secretive about them. He would cup his hand over each letter and, hunching over to one side, nod knowingly as he read.

"Just as I thought," he would say with great satisfaction and then squirrel the missive away. One afternoon I couldn't stand it any longer and I grabbed one of Lady Meredith's notes right out of Harry's hands.

"Dear Mr. Reade," it said, "Thank you for your interest. Best, Lady Meredith Davies."

"Harry, it's just a lousy form letter," I cried out, as Harry snapped the page from me.

"It's a code!" he said hotly.

It should have been a relief to have Harry safely in the hospital, but as it happened, I didn't know what to do with myself. Suddenly there was nobody I wanted to fall in love with in the Leverett house dining hall, and, as for Stu Craig, he had shown up at the room one last time, a couple days after the night Spencer and William had dragged Harry away from the Casablanca. It was about ten at night and Gus Horton, who had dropped by to ask about Harry, was just leaving. I introduced the two, and after Gus had gone Stu said with pointed sarcasm, "I suppose that's one of your *boyfriends*." Gus Horton happened to be one of the few guys in Cambridge who wasn't a boyfriend, but I wasn't letting Stu Craig in on that little detail, not if I could help it.

"That's *none* of your business," I replied grandly.

"He looks like a jerk," said Stu, and then I told him with drama that he'd really let me down that night in the Casablanca.

"I didn't know what was going on," Stu protested lamely.

"Oh, come on," I said, "I was crying and everything."

"Well, I didn't know," said Stu, and then I noticed him glance ever so slightly at his watch.

"Don't let me keep you, Stu. I've got things to do, too," I said, the things to do consisting of smoking a cigarette, and I turned away from him with a flourish and strode down the hall toward my room, hoping against hope I'd hear the patter of feet running up behind me, but instead I heard the front door quietly open and shut.

It was already November and I was, after careful consideration, supposed to have selected a major by October 3, but the only class I'd been to in a month was a Soc. Rel. course called "Humor," in which I'd simply written down everything that happened to me day by day and turned it in as a term paper. Soc. Rel. stood for Social Relations; I don't know if such a field exists now at Harvard—probably it has been replaced by accounting or something, but then it was what you took if you wanted to hang out and rap about your failed romances, except that you called them your "interpersonal relationships." It was a pretty hard course to flunk, and, once you got the vocabulary down, you didn't have to do much work, although, as opposed to a gut, you didn't admit it.

If I'd been smart, I would have picked Soc. Rel. for a major, hopeless love being my field, but instead I picked philosophy, just as Harry and I had planned, back before I realized he was higher than the moon up above. I didn't know the first thing about philosophy—I'd been too busy being thrilled that I was sitting in lecture hall next to Harry to listen to what anyone was talking about—but I figured philosophy meant talking about life, and how hard could that be?

I hadn't shown up at a single tutorial, and when I arrived at my first that November, bursting in ten minutes late, my maxi coat open and flapping behind me, I started to explain to the tutor about how my brother was crazy and had been living in my room, and the tutor had interrupted me with a "Yes, yes, we know, why don't you have a seat," so I'd felt pretty stupid. As a rule, any excuse worked on a tutor—once I told one I couldn't possibly get my paper in on time, due to social obligations—because most of them hadn't gotten into Harvard as undergraduates and consequently, if wrongly, were a little in awe of you, particularly if you were a girl wearing a teeny-weeny skirt.

Anyway, I tried to pay attention at the tutorial, but mostly I sat there fuming at this Miss D'Adamo, who'd been calling me recently in reference to my Harvard Coop bill. Generally she woke me up in the middle of a nap, for which I roundly chewed her out. What really got me mad, though, was that just the other day I'd been up at Woodward, not paying Harry much mind as he opened his junk mail, when suddenly I see popping out of an envelope a brand-spanking-new Mastercharge card, and after I'd written the Cambridge Cooperative Bank to please not send Harry another card, as he was crazy. "Thank you," Harry had said to the piece of plastic, and before I could do anything he had pocketed the card.

Plus, the class wasn't exactly what I'd had in mind. The few times I glanced up at the tutor he was writing various mathematical formulas on the blackboard of if A then B—not one whit about how many angels on the head of a pin—so I walked out before the hour was over. As I was meandering back to the dorm I heard someone coming and turned around, and there was my tutor, who was Latin American and very suave, running up to me, ostensibly to ask me why I hadn't liked the class but really to take me out for a cup of coffee. I never went back to tutorial, but I went out with the tutor a few times to these dark, subterranean coffeehouses—in those days everything was in the basement—where they put cinnamon in the coffee and charged you a dollar, until I happened to ask about the ring on his finger, and he said simply, "My wife, I love her very much."

With Harry's room standing empty in the suite, I decided, wouldn't it be great to offer it to the guy in the dorm who I had heard wasn't getting along with his roommates? The boy under consideration had blond, curly hair and was very shy and I was working at having a crush on him, even though I had never seen him close up. The brilliant idea had hit me of writing him an anonymous note that would say "Meet me at midnight at Cahaley's," and I'd had a vision of our eyes locking over the counter of beef jerky. Actually, I had stolen the idea from a story I'd heard about my grandmother and my grandfather and how she kept trying to get him to propose to her again after she'd refused him, until finally she'd written

184

him an anonymous note—"Meet me on the esplanade at five tonight"—and waited for him there in a long, hooded cloak.

"Hello, Dora," my grandfather had said to her enshrouded back.

"How did you know it was I?" said my grandmother, who was a stickler on grammar even then, and cried out, "Oh, *why* haven't you proposed to me?" to which my grandfather replied that he had and then my grandmother threw herself at his feet, saying, "But you were supposed to ask me *again!*" and then everything had turned out happily ever after—except, of course, my grandfather died six years later, but that was afterward and not part of the story. I was in the middle of recounting this to Merrill, who had promised to help me draft my note, when the phone rang.

"I've escaped," Harry said hoarsely on the other end, "and you'll never find where I'm hiding. It's on Linnaean Street." Harry hung up the phone and I pressed the button down once and called Woodward, where I got a very pleasant woman who was fascinated that I was Harry's sister and wanted to chat.

"Tell me," she said when I told what had happened, "are you as *tall* as he is?"

"Look," I shouted, "he's escaped!"

"Oh dear," she said with a sigh, "now what *are* we going to do?" I hung up the phone as the door opened and in walked Charlene, the astrologist with the Great Dane with whom Harry had lived that summer in East Cambridge. She was wearing the same black wool cape, and she walked once around the living room muttering little incantations.

"He's in my apartment and I want him out," it appeared she was saying, over and over, and then she handed me a slip of paper with an address written in what looked like eyeliner pencil. It was on Linnaean Street, all right, and it was a pretty fancy address, more than a step up from the apartment in East Cambridge, and I wanted to congratulate her on not having to spit out her toothpaste on the dirty dishes in the kitchen sink anymore, but she had already fluttered out of the room. I called up Spencer and William, and then I ran up to the Square to jump a cab.

As it turned out, I hadn't needed an address after all, because you could hear the Thelonious Monk record a mile down Linnaean.

"This is it," I said to the cabbie as I hopped out. Spencer and William were already standing there in the parking lot, accompanied by two ambulances, three police cars, and a group of bystanders that had gathered below the window from which the music was blasting. I ran to catch up with a line of policemen marching into the building.

"Don't worry," I said, jumping into the elevator with them, "he'd never hurt a fly."

The music was deafening when we got to Harry's floor.

"Let me talk to him," I told the policemen reassuringly with what amounted to a wink, and I rushed up to the apartment in which Monk was blaring and pounded on the door, which was locked.

"Harry," I called brightly through the keyhole, "it's me."

"You fucking hunk of meat, keep out!" shrieked Harry over the music. I stood up for a second, taken aback, and then, as I started to crouch down to the keyhole again, two policemen yanked me aside.

"Stand back!" one of them warned and another shot the lock off with a gun, which, frankly, I thought was a bit overdramatic. When they kicked open the door, there was Harry tossing records intently around the room.

"We've got to clean up this place, I promised I'd clean up the place," he said doggedly as he flung the LP's over the furniture. The policemen stared at him, standing in a nervous cluster by the door. I was as calm as a summer's day.

"Now, Harry," I said, taking a step toward him, but Harry gestured me back, in a way that probably looked violent from a distance, so I stepped back.

"I really fooled them this time," said Harry as he went around sweeping things off tables to the floor. He wasn't

186

wearing his glasses and he was squinting vehemently and he had a look on his face like a little boy, who having won a Pyrrhic victory, is now playing with the truck with no wheels and wondering why it isn't more fun.

"I threw my glasses and my flute in a bush so that nobody would recognize me," Harry confided to the gathering, "and then I charged a green pea jacket. I lay camouflaged in a pile of leaves the whole night. I *scarcely* dared to breathe."

I wanted to pinch his cheek, but the cops had different ideas and made me go wait downstairs. There was nothing to be frightened of, of course, but I was too tired to argue. When I got outside, I noticed the crowd had grown. For some reason it consisted mostly of old people.

"He's such a young man," I heard one grandmother type say to another, "and so generous." We heard a lot of screaming and pounding and everyone expected to see Harry emerge bound and gagged, but instead out he walked, not touching anyone, surrounded by six stricken policemen.

"I *demand* to sit up in the ambulance!" Harry shouted, as the crowd parted to let him and his retinue pass, and sure enough, the ambulance pulled out with Harry strapped in tightly but sitting up, his lower lip jutting out victoriously.

Spencer, William, and I stood watching the ambulance back up in the parking lot, then turn and drive down Linnaean.

"You love him more every time," said Spencer, and we walked up to the Square together.

Chapter Fourteen

You could almost have gotten nostalgic about Harry's escape, compared to the way he became afterward, except that all of us had stopped feeling much about anything. There had always been a crazy kind of logic to Harry's ravings, but now the last thread to reality had been broken, and Harry was left not exactly depressed but not exactly high either, just totally out of touch, as he babbled senselessly and vehemently to the black-and-white TV at Woodward, off the deep end as I had never seen him before. The parents came up, and Spencer and William and I went over occasionally, but we saw no real point in visiting every day, because there was never the slightest indication that Harry even noticed you were there, not even lifting his eyes from the TV when you first came in.

But we didn't talk about any of this, we couldn't, because we all knew inside what it was that no one was saying: that Harry might never get well again. And so we all went our separate ways—William further into blurry-eyed partying, Spencer so far into his meditating that when you looked into his eyes you saw clear-blue sky, the parents going through the motions of their life wearing stiff upper lips, and me sitting on my bed by the windowsill all night every night, smoking cigarette after cigarette and thinking intently about absolutely nothing, until the birds chirping and the garbage trucks eating garbage signaled the break of day.

The parents, who delivered moral lectures at the drop of a pin—"that was pretty slick," they'd accosted me with one morning when I was in high school, faces long with disapproval, upon discovering that I'd rerun the dishes in the dishwasher because I hadn't wanted to put them away—were silent as stone on the fact that I had allowed Harry to live with me without their knowledge. At first I had dreaded the inevitable confrontation, but when it didn't come and didn't come, I almost began to wish it had. Finally a letter did arrive from the parents the week before Thanksgiving, but it wasn't about Harry, it was about the seven-dollar check I had bounced at Cahaley's. Why my bank statement had gone to Bedford Hills in the first place and why the parents for the first and only time in their lives transgressed moral law and opened another's mail could only be explained as a cruel twist of fate. The parents' letter suggested that perhaps I ought to leave college and get a job in order to learn the value of a dollar. The parents were always trying to teach me the value of a dollar and it was always backfiring—in the second grade they had given me a quarter to save every week in some passbook savings program, with the result that at the end of the year I had a total of nine dollars, and I have not saved a penny since. The letter was in my mother's large, babyish handwriting, countersigned by my father to give it a businesslike air, and you could just tell the parents had been up all night brushing their teeth about it. My parents had the worst handwriting, but I hadn't realized how bad it was until that moment, and then I stood there getting hot under the collar, almost a decade late, about all the hubbub that had been raised about the D Miss Peron had given me in penmanship in the sixth grade ("What kind of future can you expect?" she'd asked me at the student-teacher conference), a year untarnished in

190

all other respects. The first D in the family, my father had remarked as he held the report card on that muddy March day, adding with a sigh that he guessed these things happened to people. What really got me about the letter, though, was that it conveniently overlooked the fact that Harry had been living with me for a month, and I was going to send the parents a hospital bill as a kind of ironic comment, only of course they had never wanted Harry staying with me in the first place. So, instead of opening that can of worms, I wrote them a rather lofty reply saying their letter had pained me, and left it at that.

The Tuesday before Thanksgiving my mother came up to see Harry, and afterward she came by Leverett House to take me back to Great-Aunt Elizabeth's for the night before we returned to Bedford Hills for the long weekend. She was supposed to show up at three-thirty, but instead arrived at three just as I was slamming the phone down on Mr. Kronenberg from the Cambridge Cooperative Bank—I had graduated from the weak, breathy Miss D'Adamo to the officious Mr. Kronenberg—and vowing never again to take calls from anyone who called themselves Mr. or Miss.

Her face was drawn in a way that only enhanced her looks, and she was wearing a plum-colored coat and the bright-red lipstick that was associated only with mothers in those natural-lip, heavy-mascara times, and for the first time ever, I realized how beautiful she was. My mother's looks had always defined her—"Your face is your fortune," her mother had said to her, and then used it as an excuse not to send her to college—and she had been forty before she'd dared consider she had a brain. All my life what people said about my mother was how her prettiness had taken their breath away, but I was her daughter and had never been able to see it, so engrossed was I in worrying that she was wearing large strawberry earrings or overshoes that looked like elephant feet, or whatever else I found so intensely embarrassing. I suppose I hadn't been able to judge my mother's drop-dead looks because I knew I didn't have them; even my mother, who never bragged, had once admitted she'd been more beautiful than I as a girl, though, she had always felt, with no more sex appeal than an apple, whereas I had so much *it*. I had always been so fiercely competitive with my mother, but that afternoon I was just incredibly glad to see her.

I even could have used a kiss, to tell you the truth, but I suppose it was a little late in the game to be playing at Marmee and *Little Women,* with all that running around and giving each other pats and pecks, which I had so admired from afar but had never been able to grasp the mechanics of. But then, I'd never been much good at telling her I loved her—burning up one's mother's coming-out picture in an ashtray when you're thirteen is not an especially flowery way of expressing it, I suppose. I don't actually believe I'd ever told my mother I was as much as fond of her, but then the first time I'd tried had not been encouraging. It was Christmas, and I was so young, under two, I couldn't even talk yet and my mother must have been home on a visit from the hospital. We have a picture from this period of her on the floor playing with the four of us, and I mentioned to my father when I saw it a few years ago how glamorous she looked, and he said, well, actually it wasn't a really great time for her, when you thought about it, and then I looked more closely at the photograph and saw the pained expression on her face, after she had come straight from the hospital to four children scrapping all over her to get her attention and begging for her not to leave again. Anyway, it was Christmas and I had some tenuous grasp of the concept of presents and early that morning I'd crawled down into the pantry and with trembling fingers stolen from the Hostess Cupcake packages those precious, shiny, white cardboard bottoms, which I had so coveted, then wound crumpled toilet paper around them, and deposited them in the vicinity of the Christmas tree. I had to wait through the opening of all the other presents that morning before my mother came upon the treasures. "What's this?" she'd asked, picking up one of the little wads of toilet paper, and, deciding that the one word in my vocabulary, *da-da,* would not do the trick, I'd silently watched my gifts get tossed, still wrapped, into the trash can.

In any case, I don't think the particular way I slammed down the phone on Mr. Kronenberg quite succeeded in saying "I love you" to my mother, because, instead of kissing me, my mother looked at me and said, "Haven't you gained some weight?" and it was all downhill from there.

It was my mother who had always been Great-Aunt Elizabeth's favorite, and you would often hear animated, if not exactly scintillating, stories about how during my mother's "season," she and Aunt Elizabeth, who at forty-three was nearly as popular a date as Mother, had one night decided not to go out but to stay home to wash their hair and have the maids bring them up milk toast before the fire. But then the years had passed and my brothers had grown their hair and we'd started dropping out of schools—it was these veerings from the proper way, not the nervous breakdowns, that most bothered my Aunt Elizabeth—and after that there had been little my mother could do that would not put her, as my father would say, in the doghouse.

That night we were ten minutes late to Great-Aunt Elizabeth's.

"We just assumed you were dead on the highway, so we started without you," she greeted us over turtle soup, as Uncle Win rose from the table, dressed as always in dinner jacket and black patent leather pumps, and then Aunt Elizabeth proceeded to regale us for most of the evening with tales of the wonderful Mrs. Cranmer. Before his death ten years earlier Mrs. Cranmer's husband had managed the farm for Uncle Win, and Uncle Win had taken care of Mrs. Cranmer ever since, paying most of her expenses and allowing her to continue living in the large Victorian house above the apple orchard. Mrs. Cranmer had had Aunt Elizabeth and Uncle Win to dinner the Friday before.

"And do you know, she cooked the entire dinner, for the three of us, without any help whatsoever!" Aunt Elizabeth said pointedly to my mother, though what the point was escaped us, since my mother had been cooking for the six of us without help for twenty years.

"Who *does* Lizzie look like, anyway?" Aunt Elizabeth continued, looking at me crossly. "She's not a Chittenden and she's certainly not a Greenough."

"I think Lizzie looks a bit like Ben," suggested my mother.

"*Ben?*" Aunt Elizabeth said, as if the fact of him were a startling new concept, and then turned to confide in me as if I were a disinterested party. "Southern, you know, no drive whatsoever, plays tennis with his family all weekend or slaps away at that instrument of his." She gathered herself up in her chair and called across the table to Uncle Win, "Win's never taken a day's vacation in his life, have you, dear?"

"Tried it once last year," Uncle Win told my mother on his right, "but *she* came into the library at nine in the morning and said, 'What, you still here?' and I packed up my briefcase and was out the door in ten minutes."

"Win is solid," Aunt Elizabeth repeated for the fourth time that night, "and a genius, really, when it comes to money." Not like my father, who had not gone to Harvard or even Yale. Aunt Elizabeth didn't think much of people who went to Yale, but she accepted them with a little shrug, saying she supposed people had to go somewhere.

By dessert we had passed on to a spirited discussion of the exact relationship of certain relatives to us, which saw us safely to coffee in the living room, where we spread out a copy of the family tree to see if Toby Woolcott was actually my first cousin, twice removed, or my second cousin, once removed. The clock struck ten and we thought we were home free.

But then Aunt Elizabeth said, "Went over to visit Harry today," and I imagined for a moment her sweeping into Woodward to sit staunchly next to Harry and the TV and sweeping out again. "Don't like the beard. Beards are dirty."

"I believe your father had a beard," my mother reminded her, unable to help herself.

"My father knew how to take care of *his* children," Aunt Elizabeth returned unfazed, felling my mother with this final blow as she swung into the topic of her sainted father, with whom, in actuality, she'd fought like a cat. "Home life meant something in those days. Meals like clockwork we always had and if you were a minute late for breakfast you could be sure Molly had already thrown it away in the garbage, and you went without, that's what you did, and believe me you were never late again. There was none of this running around lying dead on the highway. No, discipline, my father always said, no matter what, no matter how much you had on your hands, structured discipline. My father took care of his own investments and had three children besides, but it wouldn't have mattered if the sky blew up in his face, he made sure Molly had dinner on the table by seven." We thanked Aunt Elizabeth for the lovely time and crawled up to bed.

"You can tell how a person feels about themselves by how they treat their shoes," my mother remarked, not without insight, the next morning on the ride home, and you didn't have to be brilliant to figure out who the person was. We drove without speaking the rest of the way to Bedford Hills, my mother going exactly the speed limit and me pondering my dream of the previous night, which had begun with Richard Townsend leaving me again and continued merrily on to a kind of grade-B TV cop show, guest-starring the parents and me frantically dodging speeding vans and finally hiding out from the authorities in an abandoned warehouse.

When my father greeted us at the door with "So how's it feel to have your little girl back?" he was met with a marked

195

silence, which, however, we managed to break before dinner in order for everyone to get in a few yells about the bounced seven-dollar check.

"We're sorry our letter *pained* you," the parents said sarcastically that night, standing over me like two big kids ganging up. Their letter had also mentioned that they had given away Aphrodite, who was technically my dog, even though I, who love all dogs, was basically indifferent to her—I who can read about thousands of people being slaughtered and remain as dry-eyed as can be, but let some old dog in a book greet his master with a dry lick on the hand and I am lost for days. At any rate, the parents had handed Aphrodite over to some farmer, on the theory that, with Scout gone, she would be miserable without male companionship, reluctant as it had been. When the vet had told Mother that September that Scout had to be put to sleep, Spencer had driven down to Bedford Hills to give Scout the last rites and hold his paw as he got the shot. Spencer told me afterward he had tried to be brave, assuring Scout, as he lay whimpering and shaking on the metal hospital table, not to worry, all he was losing was his body, but after Scout got the needle, Spencer had felt the life go out of Scout's body, and he had cried like a baby. "It's all right for boys to cry," my mother, who was hipped on this subject, had said soothingly. Of course, I realize now, after all of our goings-on over Scout—me constantly marrying him as a child and dressing him up in clothes, Spencer writing poems and dedicating songs to him—that my mother was the only one of us who had always been there at six in the evening, dog food can in hand, and it was she alone who had been truly loved by Scout. But it was Spencer who cried his eyes out over the dead little black dog, and then the orderlies had come in and dumped Scout's body into a Hefty bag.

Anyway, I had been planning on making an issue of the parents' giving Aphrodite away without consulting me, but I was so taken aback by their making fun of me, I forgot.

196

The next day was Thanksgiving, and that morning, just as my mother was opening the icebox, which was crammed with cottage cheese and hamburger in case I was on the Stillman diet, and fresh vegetables in case I was on Weight Watchers, I announced I was leaving that day right after dinner.

"I thought you were staying the weekend," my mother said, with thin lips.

"I've changed my mind," I returned and marched up the stairs, hoping to crush the parents by skipping breakfast. Low tones wafted up the stairs to my room throughout the morning, murmurings punctuated by the word *she,* and then at noon George and a group of the New York cousins arrived, and it was time for the obligatory football game.

You always had to have a football game on Thanksgiving in my family, and always they dragged the women out from in front of the fire to beef up the teams. All my life I had been forced in the various seasons to play baseball or volleyball or basketball as a handicap to the team with the best players, but the game I hated the most was that Thanksgiving football, when it was bitter cold and gray and muddy, if you were lucky, and pouring rain if you were not.

I changed into baggy jeans and one of my father's sweaters and grudgingly went out onto the lawn, where I was assigned to George's team. I stood there bored as could be—I didn't have too many responsibilities, as the only thing the women were asked to do was rush forward, for some reason or another that was never explained. After the interminable chitchat about rules and boundaries, while I swayed off to one side, yawning, my hands white with cold and my feet in their maryjanes already numb, and the game finally began. At the hike, I rushed blindly forward, in a direction that bore no relation to the ball, and then my father came up and pushed me down.

My father was a very mild-mannered man, whistling through life as he polished his shoes or emptied the garbage or parked the car in the parking lot of Brookhill. When it came to sports, however, he became very competitive, still throwing his racquet at the age of sixty when one of his sons beat him in tennis, so what he had been doing at my side, so far away from the ball, was beyond me. Also, he was a nonviolent man—the one time he'd ever been sent up to spank me, I had fled to the corner of my room and shouted, "Don't *touch* me!" and he'd replied, "Well, let's just not tell your mother," and left. I was pretty surprised all around, to tell you the truth, as I sat there sprawled on the dank ground, but not as surprised as my father.

"I pushed you down," he said to me, baffled as he helped me up, "but I meant to push you down." And then he kept bringing it up during the day.

"I'm sorry I pushed you down, Lizzie," he would say, as he passed me a glass of sparkling burgundy, and then, as if he couldn't help himself, he would ruin the whole apology by adding softly, "But I meant to push you down."

Still, I felt a little melodramatic about following through with my threat to leave after dinner, but sometimes when you're being a jerk, you get yourself so tangled up you've no choice but to follow through and be a jerk to the bitter end. So, after a cold farewell I didn't mean, I got George to drive me to Stamford for the eight o'clock train and I arrived in Boston at midnight, lugging a suitcase filled with books and feeling as grimy as the sooty walls of South Station. I must have called William, because, thank God, he was there to meet me, unbesmirched by his surroundings, as always, in the ascot and herringbone jacket he had recently been donning for weekend wear.

When I got back to Leverett House I found in my mailbox a letter from Richard Townsend. It contained a friendly, rather boring report about how he was taking woodworking lessons and piano lessons and living at home. I don't think he even signed it "love." *What an ass,* I might have thought, but this would not have been convenient, for a little light bulb had gone on in my head that maybe here was a solution to things, so I bent my mind to romantic thoughts about Richard and, with an easy confidence, picked up the phone and called him in California.

"I keep expecting to see you on my doorstep," Richard intoned solemnly after we said hello.

"That's funny," I said, "because I was planning actually to be in California the week after Christmas," which was not exactly the whole truth, to say the least.

"Gee, that's great," said Richard, "maybe you could stop by or something."

The whole truth was I was going to Barbados to spend a week with Merrill and her family with a ticket my Great-Aunt Elizabeth was giving me for Christmas. Somehow, within a day, I managed to get Richard to invite me to stay with his family and Aunt Elizabeth to change the ticket to L.A. I told her I was visiting Richard's sister, and to Richard Townsend, whom I could feel panicking three thousand miles away, I wrote an ingenuous letter about how great it was that we were just friends, and that it was on that basis that I would be stopping by for a visit.

I wasn't even nervous about my plans. I knew I would get Richard back, that suddenly he had no chance against me, and I felt strong and in control again. Just to cover my bases, however, I started up meditating again. William and I, at Spencer's urging, had become meditators that October, just for something to do. For thirty-five dollars you got to sit at this lecture at the T.M. Center, where they showed you a poster of a tree and how its branches (which, you were supposed to notice, got littler and littler as they grew out) were like consciousness branching out, and then you went into an incense-filled room, and a weak-chinned guy handed you a flower and told you your mantra. I had tried to go with it, but it was hard to take the experience seriously sitting next to William, who always ruined things by applying logic. Neither of us saw a single person to get attracted to at the Center and our enthusiasm for beingness waned, until by the end of the first week our meditating had ground to a halt. I quit, I explained to Spencer, because I just didn't have the time—in the twenty minutes it took I could have smoked two cigarettes —and I can't remember the excuse William gave, although he admitted he found meditating a bit handy now and then when he had a terrific hangover.

Anyway, I took meditation up again that December because, frankly, I thought it might impress Richard Townsend. Richard was spiritual, in an incoherent sort of fashion: his mother had gotten him involved in something called The Way, and my freshman year I'd read two books by its founder, Tuni, and still hadn't a clue what it was attempting to prove.

"I-try-to-be-very-conscious-of-every-word-that-I-am-saying," Richard had droned to me the winter before, hoping to explain The Way but leaving me as much, if not more, in the dark as I had been before. And then, when I'd spoken to Richard's mother on the phone that December about my plans to visit, she'd asked, "What do you *do?*" At the time I hadn't been able to come up with much—I couldn't very well say what I did was smoke cigarettes all night long waiting for the garbage truck to start eating garbage outside my window— but later that day I skimmed Merrill's copy of *The Second Sex,* to throw a dash of women's lib into the mix, and then I called up Spencer to come over and "check" my meditation.

"We like meditating to be effortless, we try not to let the sounds around us disturb us," Spencer would say in his soothing voice as we sat cross-legged on the floor, thrilled that I had returned to the fold, yet not without his suspicions that once I had Richard back in my corner I'd be dropping transcendental meditation like a hot potato.

At any rate, though everything had changed for me—my heart sang in the mornings—nothing had changed for Harry, and I visited him a lot before Christmas, once in the dead of a blizzard, getting William to drive me in the broken-down Mercedes over to my Great-Aunt Elizabeth's to pick up the cake her cook had specially made for Harry's birthday, which fell on the same day as Beethoven's.

"Shsh, shsh!" Harry commanded some chirpy type on TV who was forecasting the weather, when William and I arrived at Woodward bearing the cake. "Uncle Hank is coming on any minute now!" and this had gone on for an entire hour, while the cake sat sprightly on the table, unnoticed.

Sometimes when I went to see Harry I would try to get his attention, but the crazier he got the sleepier I would begin to feel. I would sit there next to him and the TV, and my head would get heavier and heavier until it would fall and cradle itself in the crook of my arm, my ear against the hum of the cold Formica tabletop as if it were held to a seashell, and I would sink into a deep sleep.

I went home to Bedford Hills to spend Christmas with the parents and George before heading for California. Spencer was off with the maharishi—if you ask me, it's no accident that these meditation conferences inevitably occur during traditional religious holidays—and when I asked him what he'd be doing he said there'd be five hundred of them sitting around some place in Iowa meditating together all day long. There wasn't even a hand-woven pot holder to open from Harry that Christmas, but we had too much to be sad about to be sad, and I was so excited about getting Richard Townsend to love me again that everyone else just caught on to my mood and held on tight.

On Christmas afternoon George drove me over to Newark Airport, and I stepped on a glistening airplane that soared up into the floating clouds. I had failed Harry and now I was abandoning him, but the horrible part was, I felt great, and as the plane vanished into the sky I didn't think about Harry at all.

Chapter Fifteen

They gave Harry shock treatment fourteen times. Harry told us later how they'd taken him into a room with a bunch of beds with curtains around them, and that when he got the needle, he'd figured that was the shock, not realizing that shock was like having lightning strike you, and that you had convulsions like those cartoon characters had when they put their fingers into sockets, and that even with the sodium pentathol, it would take six people to hold him down. Harry got the shock three days after Christmas, but I didn't find out till New Year's Day, after Richard and I returned from gliding on a fake leaf boat at Disneyland, because the parents hadn't wanted to ruin my vacation.

Harry had always resisted sleeping at Woodward, screaming that he was afraid he would be hauled off in the middle of the night and given treatments—I found out later that before Spencer had left for his holiday meditation, he had written Atwood to threaten him against using shock on Harry, and although he wasn't able to recall for me the exact substance of his threat, he feared it had been something rather along the lines of don't give Harry shock treatment, or else! But the parents said the situation had gotten so bad with Harry, that Harry had actually begged for it.

I had known nothing of this as I'd driven blissfully down Sunset Boulevard in a Volkswagen convertible with Richard Townsend, and yet the instant I'd heard the parents' voices on the other end of the line I'd known what had happened to Harry, and that I could have stopped it had I been there by his side.

The parents said that nobody knew yet how shock treatment worked, when it worked, but not to worry, everything had gone well, and Harry was much quieter now and much happier.

"I had shock too, remember," my mother reminded me cheerfully over the phone, alluding to an occurrence that we had all known about, I realized at this moment, and buried in our brains, "and look at me." But I wasn't thinking about my mother; all I could think about, all I would ever think about, was what I had done to Harry.

I flew back to Cambridge the next day. The week with Richard had been gloriously hot and heavy—when I'd gotten off the plane I'd walked straight up to him and thrown myself into his arms with a long romantic kiss, which had pretty much set the tone—with Richard avowing undying love and us finally sleeping together, but after the parents' call everything had gone flat. Suddenly I felt a sick feeling inside whenever Richard touched me, a profound distaste for the merest brush against me, a queasiness so strong that when Richard reached for me I would push him away with a cry. Without the sex, there was nothing, and as Richard drove me to the airport, hitting the steering wheel in frustration from time to time with the heel of his hand, and saying he just didn't understand why I didn't love him, I remembered, remotely, all the agony he had caused me in the past, and all I could do was shake my head inside and wonder what all the fuss had been about.

After the shock Harry had been transferred to a mental

204

hospital in upstate New York, where he would be nearer the parents, so I couldn't see him for two weeks on account of exam period. Why I bothered to take exams at all when I had just decided to give up the sham and drop out of Harvard I don't know, but somehow I managed to bungle through them, even the one for the Nat. Sci. course that I had assumed would be about mollusks on the ocean floor and instead turned out to be about deciduous trees. At the time I hadn't the faintest clue what a deciduous tree was. "How can you have no scientific curiosity at all about the world we live in?" my mother was always asking, but let me say here that while it is very pleasant to walk down a tree-lined street in the fall, why do I have to know all the work that went into it? Anyway, I was hopping mad after having spent an entire night studying an old exam I'd borrowed from Linda, and by the time I got to the second question on deciduous trees, I began, "Let us turn instead to the mollusks on the ocean floor . . ." and I was finished with the test, with time to spare, by the first smoking break.

I walked back to my room to find, to my great chagrin, Richard in from California, ostensibly back East to get yet another extension on a Soc. Rel. paper due that day that he'd had a year to write. I am sorry to report that Professor Maynard was less than sympathetic to Richard's cause, and "John Updike: An Inner-Directed Man in an Outer-Directed Society" never saw the light of day, though Richard did succeed that afternoon in wheedling out of me an appointment with the family shrink so that he could discuss with her how my problems had affected our relationship.

"What relationship?" I asked, but I went with him anyway, over to Brookhill to see Rena. The three of us went into her office for a minute and then I left and waited in the lobby. After forty-five minutes Richard came out.

"I'll tell you one thing," he said as he put on his parka, "she likes you a whole lot better than she likes me."

I left Richard for the last time and went home to Bedford

Hills. I could tell the parents weren't so keen on my dropping out of school to get a job, but they couldn't say much in that it was exactly what their countersigned business letter had exhorted me to do, and I didn't say much because there wasn't much to discuss anymore except what was coming up next on TV. Spencer came back from his meditation course the second day I was in Bedford Hills and George came out from the city, and all of us, including the parents, drove upstate to visit Harry.

The hospital was a series of big brick buildings on hard, hilly grounds. Inside it was very clean, if a little shadowy— when I first saw Harry it was difficult to get a good look at him—and its hallways, high-ceilinged and cavernous, echoed your footsteps on the shiny linoleum floors. It was much nicer than Boston Rehab or Woodward, even though it was a public facility. We took Harry out to lunch to a dark, seedy bar with fluorescent fish tanks, where the lettuce was old and the salad dressing metallic, because it was the only place around. Harry's hair was still pretty shaved-looking and he didn't say much. It was the parents who did the talking, while the rest of us just sat there next to Harry, or what was left of Harry.

Epilogue

But after all of it, it was the shock treatment that worked. Not the parents trying to do the right thing, not the shrinks theorizing, not the little sister hanging around for seven years trying to help and wasting everybody's time; no, it was the mindless jamming of thousands of volts of electric current into Harry's brain that seemed to do the trick. Somehow it is so typical of life that the thing we tried so desperately to save Harry from is what seemed to save him in the end.

For it was wonderful to see Harry get better. Well, not so wonderful in the beginning, not the first few months when he moved like a robot and didn't remember things and was numb of all emotion, except for a dull thudding fear every second of the day that it was possible—it had happened to others—he might never feel anything again. And I, so horribly guilty for having let it all happen, even after Harry wrote me: "Dear Lizzie: Thank you for taking care of me when I was sick. Your brother, Harry." But then Harry was able to leave the hospital and get a job as a messenger for some Boston brokerage, and he started playing music again, and his memory started returning bit by bit until it all fell into place, everything, except for the memory of when he was crazy, which didn't seem like much of a loss, and then the music really came back, pouring out in a flood, and the next thing we knew Harry was playing with four bands at once, all of which would cancel gigs that Harry couldn't make. By the end of the year, he had quit his job as messenger and for the first time in his life was able to support himself with his music.

And Harry's still Harry, all the brain cells still there and in the same peculiar order, not crazy anymore but not exactly predictable, either. Last time I saw him he was concerned about what he would do if he was ever nominated for vice president. "I'd have to tell them I'd been manic," Harry said as he picked up his sax and started for the stage, "and then, let them do as they like."

That was almost a year ago, of course. I hardly ever see Harry now; I'm still in Cambridge, floundering about and, until recently, working unilaterally on a relationship with a comedy writer I met who was checking into Stillman because he thought he was going to swallow his tongue. It is hard to tell when you've been dropped by a guy who's afraid if he sleeps with you more than once a month he won't be funny, but when you find out he's marrying his high school sweetheart you begin to get the point. As for my career, which has for some reason gravitated to the telephone field, beginning with a job as telephone solicitor for the prestigious Time-Life Book Company, on whose behalf I sold *The Sea* and *Swamplands* as welcome additions to the coffee tables of various tired (and one blind) housewives, it, too, recently ground to a halt, when I was dismissed as Directory Assistance Operator for New England Telephone, after I calmly, but not without compassion, assured someone calling for a hospital that I was sorry, I did not find that number listed. "Some girls are not cut out to be telephone operators," Miss Birchenall consoled me at the firing, causing me to burst into tears and, I am not pleased to admit, cry out as I fled from the room, "But I got into Radcliffe," my one pathetic achievement to date and yet a fact that burns within me every time I come to the part on the application forms asking not *what* college you got into, but how many *years* of college completed, with four boxes to check —1 year, 2 years, etc.

Mother's theory is that I'm all screwed up because of the thing with Harry, but this is like when she used to say the reason I only looked at the funnies in the newspaper was because I was too worried about the fighting in Vietnam to read about it. I mean, I never worry about Harry anymore; he's practically famous now, on the road full time, and he hasn't even written.